D0992469

MUSIC IN A FOREIGN LANGUAGE

"The strikingly inventive structure of this novel allows the author to explore the similarities between fictions and history. At any point, there are infinite possibilities for the way the story, a life, or the history of the world might progress. The narrator wants to write a novel about a man and a woman who meet on a train, but is constantly distracted by his awe at the randomness of events and the number of discarded alternative stories. His ruminations are interspersed with a narrative about two friends, living in a totalitarian Britain, who are suspected of sedition. The whole work is enjoyably unpredictable, and poses profound questions about the issues of motivation, choice and morality."

The Sunday Times

"Watch Andrew Crumey, whose very different *Music, in a Foreign Language* handled real intricacies of time and ideas with astonishing maturity in a haunting, low-key up-date of 1984."

Douglas Gifford in The Scotsman's Books of the Year

"an accomplished exercise in European post-modernism."

Catherine Lockerbie

"*Music, in a Foreign Language* is complex in its change of time and points of view but entertaining, and at the same time very chilling in its convincing impression of life in a police state."

Paul Scott on Scottish Television at The Saltire Awards

"a writer more interested in inheriting the mantle of Perec and Kundera than Amis and Drabble. Like much of the most interesting British fiction around at the moment, *Music, in a Foreign Language* is being published in paperback by a small independent publishing house, giving hope that a tentative but long overdue counter-attack is being mounted on the indelible conservatism of the modern English novel.

With this novel he has begun his own small stand against cultural mediocrity, and to set himself up, like his hero, as 'a refugee from drabness. From tinned peas, and rain.'"

Jonathan Coe in The Guardian

"an intriguing and illuminating post-modern meditation on betrayal, death, and paths not taken, both personal and historical. Employing fiction within a fiction, Crumey constructs a philosophical jigsaw puzzle, partly a portrayal of an alternative, Eastern European-style post-war Britain, partly the story of the exiled narrator's life and of the characters in the novel he's writing. A promising debut from a talented and unusual writer."

The Glasgow Herald

"The main theme of this very impressive first novel is that of the falsity of both fiction and reality; and I predict that Andrew Crumey is going to be one of the major novelists who work on the boundaries between 'truth' and illusion."

Books in Scotland

Pfitz

Also by Andrew Crumey

Music, In A Foreign Language

Andrew Crumey

$\mathcal{P}fitz$

Picador USA
New York

Picador® is a U.S. registered trademark and is used by St. Martin's Press
under license from Pan Books Limited.

Library of Congress Cataloging-in-Publication Data

Crumey, Andrew, 1961–
    Pfitz / Andrew Crumey.
        p.   cm.
    ISBN 0-312-16964-7
    I. Title.
PR6053.R76P47   1997
823'.914—dc21   97-15517
                                                                      CIP

First published in the United Kingdom by Dedalus Ltd

First Picador USA Edition: October 1997

10 9 8 7 6 5 4 3 2 1

To Mary and Peter

Pfitz

Chapter One

Two centuries ago, a certain Prince sought immortality in a manner unusual even by the standards of his age. Whereas others might choose to fight glorious battles, raise monuments, or pass far-reaching laws, our Prince decided instead to devote himself to a lifelong career as the author of fantastic cities.

It began with Margaretenburg. This cherished work of his early years – the outpouring of a broken-hearted youth – was created and named in honour of the woman to whom he had been betrothed, until smallpox robbed him of her. The idea came to him as she lay on her death-bed, and within six months of her passing, all of the initial plans had been laid for her memorial. A map of the city had been constructed, displaying the perfect geometry of his conception (his reaction to the meaningless cruelty of the world), and a competition had brought forth architectural designs of the utmost splendour. Every street and building, every park and fountain would be named in memory of the woman he had lost.

Still unsure of the finer details of the proposed city, the Prince ordered a further set of charts which would show individual areas on a larger scale, and he also ordered the rendering of the intended buildings in a series of fine engravings. Landscape painters were brought from all over Europe to make illustrations of the city seen from the surrounding hills (which were themselves already being mapped, by a sub-committee of the cartographical division). At the end of this second stage (which lasted about eighteen months), the Prince felt he had come to know the city of Margaretenburg much better – to the extent that he could visit it now in his imagination, and discuss his walks with his courtiers. Nevertheless there remained many things during these hypothetical visits which were intangible and uncertain (and the Prince would not dream of commissioning any construction over which there hung the slightest uncertainty). How, for example, would the gardens smell? (a horticultural committee was formed). And would the smoke from the houses interfere with the air of the Royal Residence? (a team of eminent scientists was assembled).

This period of consultation went on for another three years. The memory of Margarete still lay heavy in the heart of the Prince, and his determination to carry on with her memorial city was undiminished; however, the cost of planning had by now placed a considerable strain on the Treasury, and it began to seem unlikely that there would be enough money left with which to begin building. A committee for finance ruled that the project could no longer remain in a state of expensive conjecture.

And yet there was still so much that was undecided. A catalogue of street plans had been compiled, and engravings of the main buildings and their interiors – but of their furnishings, there was still no more than the vaguest notion. The roads had all been named, and allocated their neat borders of trees and shrubs – but how would the fallen leaves be dealt with in autumn? And when the rains came, could anyone be sure that the drains would operate effectively? Despite all the work which had been done, the city still seemed elusive and slippery; a thing which could not yet be relied upon to come forth into the world exactly according to plan.

After much deliberation, the Prince made his decision. The city of Margaretenburg would remain a dream – a conceptual city, consisting not of streets and buildings, but of maps and illustrations. It would be a city of ideas, and as such would be a memorial more lasting than any heap of stone, since ideas alone can lay claim to immortality. All of the paperwork, in which the great city was described, was deposited in Margarete's mausoleum. And then the Prince declared that his period of mourning was over.

So it was that he completed his first work. It was now nearly five years since the tragic event which had initially inspired him, and with the closing of this chapter of his life, he felt at last a release from the long burden of his grief. Looking back, he would one day see signs of youthful impulse (even immaturity) in some aspects of the city of Margaretenburg. The mixture of styles creates clashes, dissonances (the juxtaposition of florid stucco above severe classical lines, for example, on the Lischitzky Palace). And the clock-face pattern of the streets is a conceit which would be considered unworthy of his later manner. Nevertheless, this first city showed all the signs of that irrepressible originality which one could call genius. If the strokes of inspiration were still spasmodic, then this was only through lack of practice and the skill which arises after long trial and error. All of this would come later.

The Prince became once more involved in affairs of state. He married and had three children, and it seemed that the city of Margaretenburg might be little more than a youthful folly. But during this middle phase of his career, there were to be three more conceptual cities.

Already he had created the City as Memorial. His next venture would be the City as Fantasy. Shortly after the birth of his second child, the Prince found himself in a state of malaise and dissatisfaction with life which manifested itself as a boredom with his wife, and an interest in one of the young ladies at court. He found himself dreaming of a city where he could indulge his passions to the full. Once more he assembled his team of architects and cartographers, and together they set about designing Herzchen. Things proceeded much more quickly this time – a town was conceived which had as its basis not the good order of an industrious populace (as was the case with Margaretenburg), but rather the wholehearted pursuit of pleasure. At the centre lay a great park, which was itself based on the map of the world. Its continents were lands of amusement – the Americas, where exotic caged birds gave delight and fascination; Asia, in which exquisite sweetmeats were served in the fabulous glass pagoda; Africa, which housed a wonderful menagerie; and Europe, where the well-ordered lawns would resound to constant music from a resident orchestra. Around this garden of hedonism, the remainder of the city would orbit as a mere place of rest; on the map, the great green centre bore on its periphery the yellow streets and houses like parasites on some huge lethargic animal.

Herzchen was a mere trifle, but it marked a new phase in the Prince's career as Author of Cities. There was a greater confidence now in his efforts, in contrast to the hesitant progress which he had made with Margaretenburg. When at last the task was completed, he had the book of maps and engravings locked away in a large chest (specially made for the purpose), and then he forgot all about Herzchen – along with the woman who had inspired it.

Two more cities would be founded during this brilliant middle period. Pomonia was the City as Celebration, designed to commemorate a battle which his twelve-year-old son would have fought and won, had there been a war on at the time. It was a city of fine statues, grand arches and noble barracks, and the engravings of it won fame throughout Europe, so that the Prince's unique vision became a constant subject of conversation among elevated circles. It was in answer to this new-found celebrity that he embarked on Spellensee – the City as Entertainment. Conceived as a picturesque settlement in an attractive lakeside setting, it would have as its major source of income the thousands of visitors who would come to bathe in the clear waters, and enjoy the many theatres, concert-halls and galleries. Everything was geared to satisfying contemporary taste – the most fashionable painters were commissioned to make illustrations of the works they would contribute to the art galleries; operas were similarly made to order. Coffee-houses (such as had recently become popular) would abound.

And yet it was all a disaster. Sales of the richly illustrated guidebook to Spellensee did little to cover the vast cost of the operation, and after four years of work the Treasury was almost bankrupted by it. Never again would the

Prince neglect his own artistic instincts in favour of the clamouring masses, whose interest could so easily evaporate. Spellensee became an object of loathing for him – abandoned in an incomplete and unsatisfactory state, its plans were destroyed in a fit of rage. The Prince declared that he would never create another city.

And yet, years later, he would embark on what was to be the greatest of all his projects. He was past fifty; a man who could look back on a solid lifetime's achievement which would ensure that his name would be remembered. This however, was not enough for him. The bitter memory of Spellensee still rankled – but there was also Pomonia, and there was Herzchen; and above all, there was Margaretenburg – his first work and in many ways (despite all its flaws) his best, since it was his most sincere. His career, he now could see, had been a gradual process of dilution – an almost imperceptible squandering of his talents. He had produced works which won fame, and yet had no lasting worth.

For many months he was in a state of deep depression. He neglected his duties, and his family, and chose instead to immerse himself once more in the maps and illustrations of his first city, which he retrieved from the mausoleum where they had lain.

After long weeks of solitary study and reflection, the Prince felt at last that he had found the true object for his efforts – the achievement which would validate all his earlier attempts, and provide an appropriate conclusion to his life's work. Margaretenburg had pointed the way, but he had chosen to ignore its signs; he had pursued the worldly, the concrete, the transitory and valueless. He had wasted years of his life on cities of pleasure, of hollow celebration, of facile entertainment. He would now embark on a project which would equal Margaretenburg in the solemnity of its high purpose; but this time no-one would stop him or cause him to compromise his ideals – his task would be by its very nature incapable of completion, and yet he would continue as long as his life and health allowed.

He would design the City as Encyclopaedia; a city which would provide an exposition of the complete range of human knowledge as currently understood. At its centre there would not be royal palaces, or pleasure gardens, or places of low entertainment. Instead, there would be a Museum and Library such as had never before been imagined. This alone would be enough to occupy him for a lifetime, and yet there would be so much more besides, in this great city of the imagination.

To begin with, the Prince put together an entirely new team of planners, architects, cartographers and engravers. He chose people who were young, impressionable, free from the need to preserve any reputation, and therefore willing to go wherever the task might lead. No idea must be rejected as too outrageous; everything would be subjected to equal scrutiny and consideration. And this city, unlike all the others, would be planned down to the very finest detail – nothing would be left incomplete. The cost would be enormous, but this also had been taken into account. The State itself – its entire means and all the energy of its workforce – would be directed to the one labour which would grant every citizen a place in immortality. Their own humble, mundane city (small, imperfect and inconsequential) would devour itself to create another – one which would be topographically perfect, socially harmonious, and in the range of wisdom contained within its boundaries, incapable of further addition.

Everything was sold which could attract a buyer. The Court was dissolved; its members assigned new roles in the work of planning. Only those subjects whose occupation was absolutely essential to the continued well-being of the citizenry (and hence the continuation of the Prince's plans) were spared from the project which henceforth would be the sole industry of the State. A competition was held to name the place, and was won by a Professor of Philology who proposed (for reasons which alone occupied most of the first volume of the Introductory Remarks to the City) the name of Rreinnstadt.

Laying out the streets and designing the buildings was only the smallest part of the whole enterprise. Not only every edifice, but the interior of these constructions also would have to be planned and illustrated; their furnishings and decorations, and moreover their occupants – biographies, memoirs and reminiscences would have to be written (with painstaking attention to consistent cross-referencing). There would be music and paintings for the concert-halls and galleries (not the hollow efforts of Spellensee, but works of profundity and beauty) and in addition, there would be commentaries and analyses of these works and their creators. The weather above Rreinnstadt – the patterns of the clouds, and the duration of sunlight or rainfall – all of these would have to be calculated in an operation which would break new ground in meteorology. But greatest of all, there was the planning of the Museum and Library, and their as-yet undiscovered contents.

This crucial element of the operation became, from the very outset, shrouded in secrecy and speculation. Even those who worked within the Museum Division were familiar only with those aspects in which they had direct involvement. Whether the Prince himself was able to keep track of the growth of his creation was itself a matter of debate.

The Museum's superficial appearance, on the other hand, was well known to all – a grand building overlooking a spacious square. The internal layout, similarly, would be familiar to anyone who took the trouble to examine the freely available plans – the many maps showing the locations of glass cases, of shelves, of cabinets. In the Museum, one wing was devoted to the Natural World, another to the Human. Each wing was then further divided – the Natural World being split into plant and animal; animal into flying, swimming and crawling; crawling into legless and legged, and so on in a constantly branching hierarchy of classification. Thus every beast in the world had its logical place, preserved in a case situated in the appropriate section. (One may guess that there would be

15

many empty cases awaiting the discovery of the appropriately classified animal; four-winged birds, for example, or feathered fish). The Human World was split according to an initial classification based on the five Senses and the three Faculties (memory, reason and imagination); so that paintings, for example, would be located at the intersection of two fine stairways, one leading from the Vestibule of Sight, the other from the Concourse of Imagination (via a corridor which passes through the Craft Department situated above the Hall of Touch). History, on the other hand, was reached from the Arcade of Memory (whose magnificent marble interior became the subject of a fine suite of engravings). The interconnectedness of all human knowledge and achievement would be reflected in the complexity of the internal architecture of the Museum, which came to be compared to a sponge, a crystal or a veined leaf. The ever-growing ramifications of the network of corridors and passageways soon led to countless redraftings of the interior plans and drawings, as cryptic instructions came from the Museum Division asking for the inclusion of a new route between, say, the Room of Forgotten Skills and the Chamber of Religion; or from the Mezzanine of Ambition to the Alcove of Dexterity. What these pathways may denote or imply, none could guess unless he was privy to the deepest secrets of the Museum's notional curators.

And as for the Library (which was linked to its neighbour by a system of passageways whose subtlety would extend almost beyond the possibility of symbolic representation), here there lay mysteries which were greater still. The same classification was used as in the Museum – the two buildings forming mirror images each of the other (in the engravings of the facades, the beauty of this symmetry is particularly evident). Each object in the Museum (it has been generally believed) would have been associated with a book (or several books) in the Library. However, there would also be many books which could not correspond with any exhibit (the natural history of unicorns, for example, or the geometry of round squares). The fact that these books greatly outnumber those whose function is to catalogue the exhibits next door means that the overall size of the Library (despite the density of its shelving) is equal to that of its neighbour (thus ensuring the preservation of that symmetry which was deemed so desirable by its original team of architects).

One had then (or would have had) a perfectly balanced edifice, in which everything which the human mind is capable of inventing or understanding has its place. A symmetrical complex in two halves, linked by corridors and passageways, in which knowledge can be transferred or relocated, reclassified and synthesized, simply by wandering through its richly decorated interior. One would have, in marble, glass and wood, a kind of brain, whose source of activity would be the endless perambulations of its curators, attendants and visitors. So that the city of Rreinnstadt would be not only the City as Encyclopaedia, but the City as Organism also; its central brain-like structure linked by grand roads to the watchtowers on the city walls, and the observatory in the hills beyond. An organism which would moreover have awareness of itself – for would not all those maps and plans, those biographies and engravings be included somewhere within the Library? Would the Museum not contain itself as the grandest of its exhibits?

It was a vision which makes the mind dizzy with wonder – a vision of which only our noble Prince could have been capable. It was his life's work, and also that of all his subjects, working now towards the sublime goal which he had set for them. Their own neglected houses soon fell into ruin, the roads into disrepair; food became scarce, but not paper and ink (for supplies of these most precious commodities were always ensured). Famine and epidemic could not be held back indefinitely, but their threat held no terror. For the Prince's subjects, their ultimate reward would be that great Cenotaph, erected on the central square opposite the Museum and Library, on which would be carved the name of the Prince, above those of every one of his subjects, and at the foot would be inscribed the words: 'To the memory of those who gave everything, that Rreinnstadt may live forever.'

Chapter Two

Schenck was a cartographer, and had worked on Rreinnstadt for ten years, ever since its inception by the Prince. Originally, Schenck was drafted into the Accounts Department, calculating the wages of some of Rreinnstadt's notional inhabitants. But it was observed that his penmanship was good, and so he was soon moved to the Cartography Office.

The ability to write well and copy accurately was one of the chief skills needed for his new job. Since the object of study was a city which did not exist other than on paper, the cartographer need no longer worry over such things as surveying or taking measurements. No need now for him to stand in wind and rain, his plumb line blown off course as he tries to set up his theodolite. Now it was only other maps which he would survey; his first aim being to maintain total consistency with everything which had been done before – not only the existing maps showing the simple positions of buildings and streets, but also those others which indicated height above sea-level, and others yet which showed the successive buildings, in order, which had occupied a given spot (for already by now the city of Rreinnstadt had become a thing with its own history; it had become an entity capable of transformation and development). On the shelves of the Cartography Office, there were maps of such a scale that only a single room of a single residence was shown, or a small portion of a room (every item meticulously charted and illustrated – the contours of a silver plate, or a cup upon a table; the bearings and co-ordinates of a Turkish rug spread across a floor). There were maps of finest rice-paper which could be overlaid, one upon the other, so as to show in ever-deepening layers the cross sections of the city at successive heights, and maps which indicated not only positions in space, but in time also – plans showing the location of individual citizens on particular days, at particular times (individuals whose lives were at that moment being chronicled by the Biographical Division).

It was amongst such documents that Schenck had lived and worked for the last ten years. The table from which he ate his lunch each day was an atlas placed upon his lap, and at night his dreams were laced with sweet filaments of latitude and longitude. The world itself had become for Schenck a great chart; its rich vocabulary of contours and features, a text which was completely self-contained, completely consistent, and yet endlessly perplexing. And the future which he foresaw for himself was a gradual traversing across the uncertain surface of the map, drawn at the moment of his birth, which defined his own destiny in every detail.

One day, Schenck was sent upstairs to deliver some plans to the Biographical Division. This was situated in a great high-ceilinged room, lined with galleries of shelves, amongst which the Biographers circulated endlessly, as they brought into existence the citizens of Rreinnstadt. Here was the place where new life was created; memories, dreams and speculations. It was work of inestimable importance (as the Biographers kept reminding everyone else), and when Schenck found the person he was looking for, he was curtly thanked and then dismissed as if he were no more than a servant.

Schenck made his way back along the gallery, looking down at the rows of Biographers sitting at their desks. The only sounds were those of nibs squeaking, of pens being dipped into inkwells, or of pages being turned. They even had to wear special overshoes, so as not to disturb the others whenever they needed to go and search for documents.

And then he saw her, sitting amongst the others, and it was a kind of revelation.

She was wearing green. Her hair was red, her skin pale and marked in places with a fine network of lilac veins –

marked in those places where the skin is thinnest, as for example where it stretches across the protuberance of a clavicle. This was the part which the Cartographer now watched, as she sat bent over her writing. He watched from a distance that taut area of pale skin, and the threads of veins like some hypothetical system of roads, or rivers. And he watched the thickening of the skin, its deepening, as his gaze fell southwards, beneath those chilly regions, towards the warm promise of her bosom.

If she were to lean further forwards, or else perhaps to adjust the position in which she was sitting, then he would see more. New contours would be revealed, new regions of that inviting surface. Much later, in his memory, he would compare what he saw then with his subsequent, more detailed survey.

Schenck knew that he ought to leave, now that he had completed his errand. But no one was paying any attention to him (they were always like that in Biography). And he was fascinated by what he saw; the arresting contrast of thick red hair against her white neck, and the green dress. Her pale skin called to mind a map he had once seen, of the Earth's polar regions. If she leaned further over her work, he might see more of her bosom. This hope, mingled with fear, kept him fixed in awe. He remained where he stood, motionless, his mouth dry, his stomach tightening with an excitement bordering on dread.

So that now, on the map of Schenck's life, a new feature had appeared; a snow-capped vision of mountainous beauty. And the seismic impression of this moment would send tremors to the very edges of his existence; across the distant years, he would come to recall those ridges of half-remembered dreams, gulleys of distorted memory, appearing and then vanishing again without warning. Everywhere he might choose to look on his life's map, whichever way he should turn now, he would see her indentation upon the landscape, like the hollow which remains upon a pillow after the head has risen.

Then at last she leaned forwards; aware already, he now

felt sure, of his observation. She leaned forwards, consenting to his momentary mapping of her body – or rather condescending. And as she moved, everything changed – a shifting topography of skin, flesh, mass displaced. Her breasts swelling, shrinking, falling slightly, as if in offering (only a moment!). Pendulous memory. He would think of it later, as he worked on his maps. And the question formed in his mind: how would he be able to prolong this pleasure, repeat it? How would he be able to come closer to this unknown woman who intrigued him so much?

Now she raised her head, and for a moment he was able to see her face in all its beauty, as she looked up towards the gallery. He felt her gaze discovering him, and her expression conveyed a look of quiet triumph. The Cartographer lowered his eyes, and made to leave. But by walking towards the spiral staircase at the furthest end of the gallery, he would be able, after descending its steps, to choose a route which would take him close to her desk. He prepared himself, as he began to make his way down the steps, for the imminent encounter; the brief proximity (perhaps even the possibility that he would brush against her, that some unspoken gesture would manifest itself and communicate a message of complicity, of gratitude, and the promise of further similar meetings); the narrow gap of closeness through which he had to pass – the pregnant opportunity of this moment, as he approached the object of his fascination, her head bowed once more; drew close with his eyes fixed on the door ahead, while his gaze concentrated on the mysterious figure at the periphery of his vision. And then at last he was walking past her, breathing the air in which she lived. Daring briefly to look down at her hair, and her neck, and the work before her, there were many things for him to try and assimilate in the slim wedge of time available; many pieces of information he should have liked to acquire amongst the shards of delight which were now prickling him. But from the paper on which she was writing, he could gather only a single name, spelt out in her neat blue script. *Count Zelneck.*

22

He walked on until he reached the door, and the name remained fixed in his mind as he went back downstairs to the Cartography Office; a word whose silent repetition on his lips felt almost like a kiss. It was the key which had allowed him to gain entry into a small corner of her existence; a piece of common ground now, whose investigation might bring him closer to that great act of exploration he longed so much to carry out.

Who might he be, this Count Zelneck? If Schenck could discover anything about him, then he would immediately be drawn closer to that fragrant circle which he longed to inhabit. The name seemed vaguely familiar, but this may have been illusory – like the sensation he had felt on seeing the Biographer; the profound impression that here was someone he had met before, in some other life, and whom he had known intimately, though all trace of memory had been erased. And the Count, also, seemed already like an old friend – a treasured mutual acquaintance. Schenck had to learn more about him. He decided to consult his maps.

He soon ascertained that the Count had no residence in Rreinnstadt, and so concluded that he must be one of those visitors who are regarded as significant enough (because of their status, or their links with Rreinnstadt citizens) to warrant biographical treatment in their own right. Schenck then went to the section of the Topographical Directory showing the locations of Non-Residents and Itinerants.

This was no easy feat. The Section (in four volumes) contained a huge number of maps, on which were indicated (amongst other data) the positions of individuals within Rreinnstadt at various times, over a period covering several years. To find one person amongst this transient crowd would be impossible, without some further clue to his possible whereabouts.

But luck was on the Cartographer's side. Later that day, he was in the Map Room when he met Gruber, who was looking for a road plan giving indications of traffic at the time of the Festival of the Swan (the great annual celebration which attracted large numbers of visitors to Rreinns-

23

tadt from the surrounding country). Gruber said that someone in Biography had requested it, and Schenck saw an
opportunity to pay another visit to the solemn place upstairs
with its intriguing treasures.

'Thanks for offering,' said Gruber, 'but I'd rather take it
myself. It's a pretty piece of work who wants it.'

Schenck was filled with excitement and agitation when
he heard this; the very suggestion of the woman he longed
to see again made her seem as vivid as if she had walked
into the room. But also he was seized by jealousy at the
thought that Gruber might be about to beat him to his
goal. He had to satisfy himself that Gruber was actually
referring to another biographer. 'What's she like?' he
asked.

'Redhead. Just my type.'

He would have to act quickly. There was no chance of
delaying Gruber, but he could at least try to obtain as
much information as possible without letting Gruber suspect his intentions.

'Let me help you. Exactly what date does she need?'

Gruber told him the day and year, and even explained
that the Biographer was planning Count Zelneck's journey
from his country seat, wishing to avoid those roads which
would be most congested with travelling peasants and
vagabonds.

'Here it is,' said Gruber, who had found the map he was
looking for. Then he began to flatten his hair with his
hand, and straighten his cravat as he walked out with the
book under his arm. 'See you later!'

Schenck felt sick at the prospect of being usurped by this
oaf. But at least he knew now the exact time of Zelneck's
visit. He returned to the Directory, and studied every chart
of Rreinnstadt for the appropriate day. Finally, after more
than an hour of frantic searching, he found the Count.

There he lay, on a map of the Tischner Quarter of
Rreinnstadt on the first morning of the Festival of the
Swan. It was a map set in the early morning, the sun
hardly risen, and everyone still asleep, save a few insomniacs

24

who were marked, their names minutely inscribed, in the streets and parks where they walked. Spurned lovers, perhaps, or dazed revellers, or possibly even criminals (who had already, at that time, begun to appear in Rreinnstadt). And in a tavern on Schlessingerstrasse (how many such taverns Schenck had previously searched!), in an upstairs room, the pale blue rectangle showing the bed in which the Count lay. Her Count. Looking at that neatly drawn symbol, it was as if Schenck were gazing straight into the Biographer's own heart. And he thought once more of that fascinating rectangle of neck and bosom, that perplexing map of a territory whose features had been represented to him in a code which he was still attempting to decipher, as he reworked its memory again and again.

Schenck almost wanted to pick up the book and hug it. Here was the Count – here was the beginning of his entry into the Biographer's life, her world. At this moment, she too was thinking about the Count – weaving the fabric of his existence, bringing together the events which would shape him; deeds of heroism or nobility which might mould him, memories he would carry with him as he made his journey towards that bed where he would sleep, in a Rreinnstadt tavern, on the morning of the Festival of the Swan.

Everything about this tavern was now fascinating. He consulted other maps, found the floor plan of the building; studied its every detail, explored the rooms in which the Biographer too might find herself, once she had brought her Count to his destination. And he studied over and over that chart which showed him sleeping in his bed, and all the other Non-Residents and Itinerants; the beggars in the parks (marked in grey), and all the additional topographical detail, minutely encoded. A pile of leaves, soon to be blown away. A beer barrel – fallen from its wagon – cracked and spilled across a street. The beer (symbolically) lying uncleaned in that early morning, and giving off its beery fumes to the sleeping citizens (this malodorous cloud being of ill-defined extent, its representation being decoded in the marginal Key). Even the roaming dogs were frozen in their tracks, marked by tiny crosses.

And the tavern, its guests located and named. The Count was not alone in his room. On the floor beside him Schenck saw an irregular figure of roughly human proportions, erased and redrawn, along with a pencilled inscription which Schenck could not easily decipher. Pfitz, it looked like. This must be the Count's servant. And the Cartographer felt even greater joy, that his researches should have taken him slightly further into the life of the Count.

But what about Gruber? Schenck had not seen him again; he could only speculate on the kind of success which he might already have achieved with the Biographer. For the rest of the day, he pursued his work with a troubled heart – contours were badly drawn, bearings misnumbered. He could think only about the Count, and Pfitz, and the lovely Biographer.

As evening approached, Schenck packed his things and began to make his way back to his lodgings. He followed the streets blindly as he took his usual route, hardly noticing the waggoners, the flower sellers, or the couples walking arm in arm. But as he came past the iron gates of the park, he was brought rudely from his dreams. At the far end of the street, he saw Gruber and the Biographer. She must have agreed to let him walk her home. Schenck began to follow, trying to ensure that if either of them should turn he would not be seen. In any case, it was already growing dark, and the two figures up ahead seemed too engrossed in their conversation for there to be any chance of them looking back. Schenck cursed his bad luck. If only he were in Roads and Thoroughfares, instead of those cursed Aquifers, then it would have been he, not Gruber, who would have been charged with finding the Biographer's map. And then it would be he who was walking beside her now, feeling her delicate arm in his.

As he followed, his attention remained fixed on the two figures ahead; their closeness, the symmetrical motion of their limbs, their swaying bodies as they walked slowly together, like reeds in a common current. He fancied that he saw the death of all his dreams. Yet still he followed them, along successive streets. What did he hope to discover? Would he eventually find himself standing in misery beneath a window in which he would see their two figures embrace?

They were in a dark alley now, lined with tall overhanging houses. It was not one of the better areas of the city, and Schenck might have felt nervous to walk here, were his attention not so preoccupied with the couple who went before him. There was no one else about, nor was there any traffic, and so Schenck gave a start when he heard and then saw a carriage speed past him. It was going far too quickly for such a narrow street – and as it approached Gruber and the Biographer, Schenck saw its wheel mount the pavement. They would be hit! Everything happened too quickly for Schenck to have to decide whether to call out in warning. Already the high wheel of the carriage had pushed Gruber off his feet and against a wall; he was lying on the ground, cursing loudly at the escaping vehicle, while the Biographer was helping him to get up again. Mingled with shock, the Cartographer felt a malicious pleasure at the sight of Gruber, a ridiculous figure brushing the dirt from himself and limping with aching limbs. Gruber did not appear to be seriously hurt, but he and the Biographer were in danger now of looking round and seeing Schenck – perhaps even suspecting his involvement (such was Schenck's delight, that he felt somehow responsible). Schenck quickly went back to the corner of the street, where he turned out of sight. As he walked briskly back to his lodgings, he congratulated himself that the random motion of a badly driven carriage had made Gruber look comical and absurd, spoiled his plans, and given new life to Schenck's hopes.

Chapter Three

Next morning, Gruber did not come to work. His arm was too painful for him to be able to write. Schenck felt sorry for him now, but could easily afford to, since the accident had simultaneously removed an obstacle and provided an opportunity. The maps had not yet been returned from the Biography Division (Schenck had checked). He could go and ask for them back.

Schenck prepared himself very thoroughly for the encounter. He thought about the manner in which he would approach her desk, the way in which he would attract her attention and make her look up and notice him. Not a cough or gesture of awkwardness – he would speak to her clearly and confidently. He rehearsed it in his mind: 'Excuse me,' or 'Excuse me, miss.' Or 'Good morning.' The last formula seemed the most powerful, the most business-like. 'I believe you still possess certain charts . . .' And during their conversation, he would be observing her, gauging her reaction, assessing the various possibilities.

But what if it were all to go terribly wrong?

After two hours of vacillation, Schenck felt ready to carry out his mission. Any further delay, and the maps might be returned before he took his chance. He went upstairs, and found himself once more in the biographers' silent citadel. The woman he sought was sitting at her desk, with her back to him. He savoured the view he had as he approached, of the firm curve of her shoulders, and the bare nape of the neck which was exposed by her tied hair. And then he was standing beside her desk, and she was showing no sign of having noticed him.

It seemed that all his resolve, all his firm confidence, had magically evaporated in the few paces which had taken him from the door to his present position. He waited, hoping that she would look up. He even tried to read what was on the paper before her. Eventually he forced himself to speak, but what emerged was an embarrassed squeak which he found it necessary to disguise as a cough. The Biographer looked up at him sternly, and so did everyone else in the quiet room. Simply to speak to her was hard enough, but now Schenck felt that he was addressing the whole company; all of her colleagues and friends. He longed to run away, back to the safety of his maps.

'I've come to collect a chart. You borrowed . . . It was brought . . . Last night. I mean, yesterday.'

She had already pulled the volume out from under a pile of other books. Schenck noticed how strong her arms were.

'This one?' She was holding it up for him to take. The rest of the biographers had lost interest in him now.

'Yes. Thanks.' He took it from her, and felt its great, stubborn weight. Was this the best he could do? Must he now turn and leave? Already she was returning to her writing.

'I understand you're working on Count Zelneck?'

'That's right.'

She had a fascinating mole below her left ear. When she spoke, it was with the confident *ennui* which only exceptional beauty can bring.

'And his servant, Pfitz?' Schenck said this so as to sound knowledgeable – he said it so as to suggest to her that already he had infiltrated a realm which she regarded as her own. He said it, because there was nothing else he could say, and the only alternative was to leave.

'Pfitz?' she replied. 'I know of no such man.'

Schenck was taken aback by this. Had she perhaps not gone far enough into the Count's life to discover this other character? But he persisted. He wanted her to understand his great knowledge of the Count, which might be so useful to her later on. And so he continued:

'I worked on the map which shows the tavern where the Count will sleep during his visit. Pfitz lies beside him.'

Still she looked confused, and now even a little anxious.

She was pushing and prodding the heavy books which littered her desk, as if searching for their support. 'I've never read anything about Pfitz. I must have overlooked his existence . . .'

Now he could see his chance to strike. 'But Pfitz is the Count's most faithful servant – the two are inseparable. I'm sure I came across something in the Department of Anecdotes . . .'

'Do you have a reference? I must see it.'

'I can easily go and check the matter out. Leave it to me.'

She smiled with relief, indebted to the Cartographer for the assistance he had offered. Schenck felt dizzy with joy at the unexpected success of his bluff.

'Find me whatever you can,' she said, 'and bring it to me. I should be most grateful.'

There was so much more that he wanted to discover. Who was this woman? What was her name? But he would have to be patient. He had his excuse now to see her again. He took his leave, and went back downstairs, the steps beneath his feet feeling light as clouds.

Bluffing was all very well, but now Schenck had to come up with some information on Pfitz. He first tried the General Catalogue, but the name was not there. This was not so unusual – the humble servant of a visitor would not be likely to have an entry. So Schenck next decided to find out who was responsible for the map on which Pfitz was shown.

His enquiries led him to the team of Illustrators and Letterers within the Cartography Department. The elderly clerk squinted at the crisp map which was unfolded beneath his eyes.

'Hmm. It has something of Hubert's style, though without his easy manner – these contours show a hesitancy which would be quite foreign to him. The hatched areas here are reminiscent of Albrecht . . . I'm not sure, though. And the lettering,' he peered through his thick reading lenses, 'would seem to be in the hand of Herr Balthus.'

Schenck asked if he could see this Herr Balthus.

'I'm afraid he passed away, a little over a year ago.'

That was no help. Schenck next tried the Index of Casual Remarks, in the Department of Anecdotes. Had anyone ever mentioned the name of Pfitz? Still he could find nothing. It seemed that apart from his presence in the tavern, Pfitz was invisible and unknown. And yet he was there on the map, on the floor beside Count Zelneck. Badly drawn and poorly labelled, but a man nevertheless.

What was he to do? Should he go back to the Biographer and tell her that he had failed, or been mistaken? At best, she would give a contemptuous shrug, and the link that had been established between them would be broken forever. Schenck needed Pfitz, in order to maintain some fragile contact with the woman whose name he still did not even know.

In the Portrait Office – nothing. The Police records had never heard of him, nor any of the Guild archives. Where had Herr Balthus found him, when he entered his name on the map? In desperation Schenck tried the Office of Missing and Displaced Persons, where an elderly lady spent so long trying to find some reference to Pfitz that the Cartographer feared his own absence from his desk was bound to be noticed, and he himself would become the subject of a search party.

But when he returned, he found business carrying on there in its usual sleepy way, his truancy having gone unnoticed. Schenck laboured despondently over his maps. He had found such a perfect opportunity to work with the Biographer – to run errands for her, help her in numerous ways, begin to learn her heart's secrets. If only he could find Pfitz.

The day drew to a close, and he went home without being any closer to discovering the mysterious character who might hold the key to winning the Biographer's affection. When he reached his lodgings he was met by Frau Luppen, his landlady; a woman of firm principles and considerable proportions, who had begun recently to show an unwelcome interest in the welfare of her lodger. Frau Luppen asked Schenck if he had eaten, and before he could answer, commanded him to join her for dinner, since – she said – he looked like he needed fattening up a bit.

Her husband had died many years earlier; some said of exhaustion, others suggested an accident involving the injudicious distribution of his wife's weight one night. Eating the stew of cabbage and pigflesh which was placed before him, Schenck considered other possibilities.

'You're very pale these days, Herr Schenck, and you look like you're wasting away. You're not *en amour* are you?' When Frau Luppen giggled, the dimples creased and sank into the depths of her cheeks like lost islands.

Schenck did not know what to say. As he listened to the words of his landlady, and looked at the fatty lump of pigflesh – still bearing stubbly hairs – which his fork had discovered, he could think only of the Biographer, and all the great barriers which he had to try and overcome.

From the floor behind him, Schenck heard a sudden yapping. It was Frau Luppen's pet dog, a long-haired creature no larger than a rat, and with a pink bow tied on its head.

'Flussi, don't shout now. Come to mummy.' The dog skidded across the floor, then jumped up onto its mistress's lap. She licked from the edge of Frau Luppen's plate while the landlady pursued her train of thought.

'What you need is a good woman, Herr Schenck. I can't understand how a nice man like you can't find a wife. Just not the marrying type, I suppose, is that it? Let them fall in love with you then break their hearts. But ah! what a lovely thing it is to be young. Here you are, Flussi.' She helped her pet to a piece of meat, and Schenck watched her plump arms, dimpled at the elbows. This was a creature just like the Biographer, yet how different! Her pink arm reaching across her breast, stretching over the mountainous expanse of her bosom. Her neck, deeply creased, and the tight ringlets of her hair, so carefully applied. She looked up at him, and it seemed as if she blushed, so that Schenck also felt uneasy. He put his fork's catch straight into his mouth, and felt pig-stubble against his palate.

'You're even losing your appetite. You aren't ill are you?' Frau Luppen got up and placed the back of her hand against Schenck's cold forehead. She left it there a moment, trying to detect a temperature. 'The best way is to use the cheek instead of the hand, of course.' She giggled again. 'But that might be taken the wrong way.'

Schenck imagined her cheek against his forehead. A great pillow of flesh. He imagined himself sinking into those dimples and being lost forever. And then he saw again the Biographer's stern gaze. 'Thank you so much for the meal, Frau Luppen. But you're right, I'm a little unwell. I shall go to bed early tonight.'

'Are you warm enough up there?'

'Yes, perfectly. Thank-you. Good night.' The dog yapped. 'And good night to you, Flussi.'

Frau Luppen tugged at the dog's paw. 'You see, she's waving at you!' It looked as if she might even be trying to make the dog blow a kiss. 'Good night, Herr Schenck. Don't let your work tire you out.'

Upstairs, in his small room, Schenck sat down at the table by the window and looked out into the darkness. Where was she? Where was Pfitz? Tomorrow he would have to continue his quest – what if he were to fail again? How long would he have to search, before admitting defeat?

Then Schenck was hit by a stroke of inspiration. Since his research had yielded nothing, might he not resort instead to artifice? He could compound bluff with further bluff. What was there to prevent him from inventing Pfitz's story himself? He could present it as a work of fiction, borrowed from a copyist in the Literature Division, and based – perhaps only loosely – on the true person. It would be little more than a delaying tactic, but it would win him another interview with the Biographer. Thrilled by his own cunning, Schenck got up and lit the lamp, then sat down again with a full inkwell before him, and a sheaf of paper. And so he began to make up the story of Pfitz.

Chapter Four

Pfitz and his master, the Count, are preparing to ride on towards the great city of Rreinnstadt.

COUNT: (seated on a hillock, and struggling to pull on his boot). Confound the thing!

PFITZ: Do you want me to help you?

COUNT: No, I prefer to wrestle with it myself. That way I shall have more satisfaction when I eventually manage to put it on. Are the horses ready?

PFITZ: Their harnesses and saddles are, but as for the horses themselves, you'd have to ask them. Personally, I suspect not, but they always do as they're told.

COUNT: (still struggling). Confound and damn this boot! (He stands up, the heel bending under the foot which is not yet fully inside.) Look at me – like a cripple. Perhaps if I stamp enough it'll go on properly.

PFITZ: That's it – stamp, stamp, stamp until you get what you want. Then blame the boots for being too small when it's your feet that are too big. Are you sure you don't want any help?

COUNT: There, at last! Now let's mount and go on our way. Do you think we'll get there today?

PFITZ: Neither today, nor tomorrow, nor the day after that.

COUNT: It's not so far, surely?

PFITZ: It isn't distance that I'm thinking about. As my father used to say, the longest journey of all is the one which takes you nowhere.

COUNT: And what the devil did he mean by that?

PFITZ: I've no idea. But since he was a very wise man it must have some depth to it.

The Reader will have noticed that there has been no mention so far of the physical appearance of Pfitz and his master, nor any indication of their ages. This is a deliberate decision on the part of the Author. Since he never met either the Count or his servant personally, and was unwilling to rely on the conflicting testimony of those who have tried to paint in words the evidence of their unreliable memories, the Author has decided to omit such speculations entirely.

– But if the Author has never even met Pfitz and the Count, then how can we be expected to believe anything which he tells us about them?

Because the Author assures us that every word of it is true, and since he is an honourable man (or so I am told), we shall just have to take his word for it.

Pfitz and his master ride in silence for some time. At last, the Count speaks.

COUNT: Say something Pfitz, to ease the boredom.
PFITZ: Isn't the countryside sufficiently interesting for you?
COUNT: You know how I loathe the countryside. Every tree and bush only reminds me how far I am from civilization. Tell me a story.
PFITZ: Do you want a serious one or an amusing one?
COUNT: You choose.
PFITZ: Long or short?
COUNT: Just long enough to reach its end.
PFITZ: And do you want it to have a moral in it?
COUNT: What could you ever teach me about morals?

The Reader will also have noticed by now that in presenting his account of the two travellers, the Author has avoided those lengthy passages of narrative in which florid language is used so as to dress up and pad out a lack of interesting events. He could, for example, have told us a great deal about that boot which the Count struggled a little earlier to put on – he could have told us where it was manufactured, and how it had served the Count through numerous battles and adventures. He could have spent three pages or more on the putting on of that boot; the vainly repeated attempts, and the sensations of crushing and squeezing which the foot meanwhile endured. There are many other Authors who would choose such an approach (and many Readers who would prefer it), however our Author is not one of them.

By now, Pfitz had finished his story.

– That's not fair! I wanted to hear it!

Then you should have been listening to Pfitz, instead of to me.

COUNT: Well told Pfitz, and a surprising ending. Do you think we've got much nearer yet to the next village?

PFITZ: Doesn't seem like it. Hard to tell, when everywhere is so similar.

COUNT: That's the trouble with the countryside – all looks the bloody same.

They ride on further, along lanes which need no description since they look just like any other lane. And the countryside through which these two characters travel is something which the Reader is free to construct in any way which seems appropriate. After all, when a theatre is putting on a play, it uses whatever props are available. A tree will appear in a Shakespeare comedy, and then again the following week in Corneille; a dagger will make as many different entrances as there are dramas requiring it to perform its part. And whenever you read a description of the countryside, you must construct, from the mental props available to you, something which will fit well enough with the words on the page. Naturally, any text which is too much overburdened with details will put at a disadvantage those Readers who have only a limited supply of mental furnishing (for whatever reason). It is therefore in a spirit of fair play, and so as to put all Readers on a completely equal footing, that the Author will avoid the unfair device of such 'descriptive' writing.

– But I like to read descriptions! I want to have a scene painted before me, which I can enter into.

Those scenes exist only in your head. You think a book is good because it reminds you of things you already know. And what's the point of that?

COUNT: Tell me, Pfitz, what will you do when we get to Rreinnstadt?

PFITZ: I shall serve you, of course, same as always.

COUNT: No, what I mean to ask you is whether you have any intention of seeing the sights of the city, or its taverns. Its women, perhaps?

PFITZ: Lets just see how it goes. As my father always said, the best plan is no plan.

COUNT: I take it from that, that you were an unintended child?

PFITZ: All children are unintended. Their parents may want a child, but they can never want the particular child whom they get, since they don't know what they'll get until they've got it.

COUNT: There are some children, though, whose conception can only be termed an accident. Were you perhaps one of those?

PFITZ: Everything in this world happens by accident. The circumstances in which I was conceived were no exception.

COUNT: I should like to hear about it.

— Wait a moment. Before we carry on, could I at least have the right to reply to what you said to me a minute ago? I think it's very presumptuous of you to say that I only like books that remind me of what I already know. It so happens that I like books which can teach me things, and so far I haven't learned anything from this one!

Please dear Reader, can you stop all these interruptions and let us continue?

— Don't call me 'dear'. I won't go a step further until you let me have my say. Already we've lost one of Pfitz's stories because you talked all the way through it. Why don't you let him tell it again?

But Pfitz is telling his second story now — you can't expect him to tell two stories at the same time, surely? If you like I can summarize it for you . . .

— No! I want to hear it from Pfitz, or not at all.

37

Already the journey of Pfitz and his master has met its first obstacle, as our Reader stops by the wayside, complaining loudly. I can hear her saying something about language, and description, and narrative voice, and that books are supposed to be about the realities of life, and feelings, and characters who develop through the events which occur to them. Now someone else is saying something to her – I think he's saying that a book which only portrays the world as we already believe it to be is no better than the poorest entertainment. He's saying that the purpose of a book is not simply to go from one place to another, from a beginning to an end, all the while holding pictures up and inviting the audience to believe that they are real. But she isn't happy with this, she's pouting and stamping her foot. How can we continue without a Reader? Won't you come with us just a little further?

– Only if the Author can convince me that his work has got something to do with the real world.

The Author says that if his story is to resemble the world in any way at all, then it must be formless and without logic, proceeding randomly from one moment to the next. Then gradually, patterns will emerge which may or may not indicate events, ideas or actions. People will appear who may turn out to be crucially important, or else they may vanish after a single night, never to be seen again. And then, just when you think everything's got going, it'll all suddenly stop.

The Author says also that if his story is to resemble the world at all faithfully then he will not attempt to burrow inside the heads of his characters, and attribute to them thoughts and emotions of which he can have no knowledge. Instead, he will report their behaviour and their speech in as honest a manner as he is able. Nor will he clutter his pages with elegant description, since the world is made of things, not words, and to try and capture reality in words is as meaningless as trying to make a butterfly out of sand.

Now can we proceed?

– Only if you let me hear the story of Pfitz's conception!

Very well, with the Author's permission, we shall turn back as far as the story of how it was that Pfitz came to be born.

PFITZ: My mother came from a little village in the country, the sort of place where nothing ever happens. One day a travelling fair visited – it was a huge event for the village, and a big adventure for my mother. She was sixteen at the time and had never seen anything like it. In the evening she put on her best dress and after a lot of pleading her parents allowed her out.

The fair consisted of the usual collection of rough tents and wagons. There was a fire-eater and a juggler, and a bear on a chain. But what caught my mother's attention was a larger tent, outside of which a crier was announcing the forthcoming performance.

'Roll up! Roll up! Come and see Fernando, the incredible Bee-King.'

My mother didn't know what this could possibly mean. She gave her money to the crier, then went in to join the rest of the crowd inside.

Half the village were in there, sitting on benches or standing shoulder to shoulder, all trying to see the small stage which had been put up behind a curtain of fine gauze. Some whispered that he was a magician, others that he was a freak. All had heard that his act was unlike anything else in the entire world. And then there he was, standing on the stage behind the gauze; a tall, elegant man with brilliant black hair, gleaming teeth, and a pencilled moustache. Fernando, in a long cape, with a glass box containing his collection of performing bees.

That's right, performing bees. Don't ask me how he made them do it, but out they came, one by one; fat bumble-bees, the kind that seem almost too heavy to fly. At first it was straightforward stuff, flying through tiny burning hoops and so on, while the audience watched through the gauze which protected them from Fernando's strange menagerie. He produced some with little pieces of paper stuck to their bodies, so that they looked like angels, or floating clouds. Three of the bees were connected together with threads to look like a horse-drawn carriage going through the air. Fernando wasn't at all afraid that they might sting him – he even made one fly in and out of his open mouth, gathering pollen from his tongue. Finally, as the climax of the performance, there was a magnificent mock battle, in which two armies of uniformed bees clashed and swirled in a great crescendo of buzzing. The crowd went wild, and the show was over.

After everyone had dispersed, my mother still hung around outside the tent, amazed and awe-struck by what she had witnessed. Then she saw Fernando come out from the back, dressed now in an ordinary, shabby tunic. 'Did you really make them do all those tricks?' she said. 'Were they real bees?'

Fernando was charmed by her naivety. 'Yes, of course,' he said. 'I'm glad you enjoyed the show,' and he started to walk on.

But she called after him, 'Please wait,' and when he turned round she didn't know what to say; she just looked down at her toes.

Fernando came back towards her, put his hand under her chin and gently raised her face. 'There is one very special trick,' he said, 'which I don't normally include in my act for the general public. Would you like to see it?' And he led her back into the tent.

Once inside, he lit the lamps again, and positioned himself behind the gauze. He brought out the glass box full of bees, placed it carefully on the table before him, and lifted the lid. Then he stood back, stretched his arms wide, and raised his proud face in readiness.

They were beginning to fly out; only a few at first, but soon there was a great swarm of them buzzing in the air, some with their little paper angel wings still attached, a great swirling cloud of stirring bees. And they were all flying towards the head of Fernando, circling and landing, crawling and searching. A mass of them was forming on his face, his hair; a great beard of them hung from his chin, and the place towards which they were all moving, as if led by some unseen force, was his open mouth. They were jostling on his tongue; some were pushed aside and would fly back to try again. In they were all going – hundreds, thousands of them into the mouth of Fernando and down his throat into their human hive, so that you could hear them humming inside. And within the open mouth, it was not pink flesh which my mother could now see, but the glowing yellow wax of a honeycomb.

She ran out screaming, through the crowds which still thronged around the other attractions, screaming all the way home, refusing to say anything of what she had seen. In the morning, Fernando and his tent and his box of bees were gone.

COUNT: (laughing). I don't believe a word of it. And anyway, I thought you were going to tell me how it was that you came to be born.

PFITZ: Ah yes sir, so I was. Well, six years later my mother moved to the city and married a glazier.

It had begun to rain. They took shelter under a tree. After a while the rain stopped.

– What was the point of telling me that?

The Author only mentions it because it really happened. And look, you've got wet now. There are spots of rain on your sleeve. Let me wipe them . . .

– Don't bother. Let's have more of Pfitz's story.

COUNT: Then how did you come to be born?

PFITZ: I told you; it happened by accident sir, just like everything else in this world.

COUNT: Is that really what you believe, that everything is an accident? Even our own thoughts, perhaps?

PFITZ: It's what my father always used to say, and I've no reason to disagree with his wisdom.

They hear a gentle bump on the ground beside the road. An apple has fallen from a tree. Pfitz gets down from his horse to pick it up.

PFITZ: And just when I was feeling peckish! Try telling me that this wasn't a piece of pure chance.

COUNT: The apple fell at that moment simply because the laws of gravity and mechanics dictated that it should. It fell then because it could not have fallen a moment sooner or a moment later.

PFITZ: But why was I here to pick it up?

COUNT: Because the laws which govern the motion of apples also govern the atoms in your body and your brain, and all of these things moved in such a way as to bring you to this place at this time. They made you decide to follow me here, and they made you feel hungry, and they made you get down off your horse. Your life is as completely determined as the course of a falling apple. Every event has a cause, and every cause is itself the outcome of some previous event. If you take the chain back far enough, you will find that everything which happens in the world does so because it is logically necessary for it to occur.

PFITZ: Try telling that to my father! I'm sure he didn't think that way when he made me.

In truth, this debate is one in which Pfitz and the Count engaged on many occasions. For not only had the Count taught Pfitz to read, but he had then made him study the works of all the great philosophers, in order that master and servant might pass the time in stimulating discourse. Thus it was, that Pfitz came to know Plato and Aquinas, Spinoza and Locke. But at the end of it all he still agreed with what his father used to say, that nothing in this world is ever black and white.

— But was it not the Author who made the apple fall?

42

And the story of Pfitz's entire life must already be determined, since the Author knows from the outset how it will all end.

Then what of your own life, Reader? Is that a story which has already been concluded in the mind of its own Author? There are some who believe that the world itself is no more than a great book, written up above by an unseen hand, and our lives are nothing but the gradual reading of a fate which has existed for an eternity before we are even born. And there are some who believe that our life is only one of several possible books in a great library, and we shall never know which book was that of our own life until we reach the final page (by which time it will be too late to do very much about it). Still others assert that the books themselves are being written as we speak, and their plot is something over which we can have some influence. It is a matter of debate within that particular school, whether the way in which those books turn out was already dictated by some higher book, in some higher library, or whether indeed there may be an infinite hierarchy of books and libraries governing the fate of coincidences, the coincidences of fate, the fate of fates, or the coincidences of coincidences.

– Sir, are you trying now to seduce me with philosophy?

Perhaps it is written up above that this is what will happen.

– We shall see.

COUNT: But if I were to take your apple in my hand and then drop it, it's surely no accident that it falls to the ground?

PFITZ: Just because apples have always done so in the past doesn't mean they will continue to do the same for all time. What if one day you should release an apple and see that it flies up into the air like a bird?

COUNT: Then I should conclude that either I am mad or that the apple was not really an apple at all . . .

PFITZ: In which case apples fall only by definition . . .

COUNT: Or else I should have to conclude that the law of gravity had been violated.

PFITZ: And does nature habitually follow this law out of some sense of the common good, perhaps?

COUNT: I don't know. It just does.

PFITZ: Then your account of the logical reason why an apple should fall is that it 'just does'. And we could equally well imagine a world in which it 'just doesn't'. Is there any particular reason, then, why we should have happened to find ourselves in this world and not in some other?

COUNT: Well I am perfectly happy to exist in this world, Pfitz, for all its faults and shortcomings; and I hope that I shall continue to exist here for a very long time. You imagine a world which is chaotic, random and meaningless – but what about the great achievements of scientists and astronomers? What about Mr. Newton, and his explanation of the mechanisms which drive the universe? Already, they've nearly got the whole thing sewn up. Just give them a few more years, while they tie up the loose ends, and then we (or rather they) will understand the ultimate laws of nature. We'll truly know the mind of God.

PFITZ: Now that would be very interesting indeed.

COUNT: But I'm still no nearer to learning the story of how it was that you came into the world.

PFITZ: Perhaps not, but we've managed to get ourselves a little closer to Rreinnstadt in the meantime. Have patience, sir. I shall tell you the rest later.

Chapter Five

How long it takes, to write a tale which may be read in a few minutes! It was only the thought of the Biographer which sustained Schenck, as he invented the first part of Pfitz's story, but at last he collapsed in exhaustion over his work. When he came to, he found himself still fully clothed at his desk, and with the pale light of dawn creeping over him.

To rise without having had the benefit of sleep is a disorientating experience. His mouth was dry, his limbs aching, and he had the feeling that he was no longer himself, but was instead watching the movements of a stranger. The man who has gone without sleep finds himself in an unfamiliar, pallid world; the quiet street below his window shaking itself into its first secret rituals of the day, and always in his head the incessant dizzy numbness, the feeling of nausea bordering on euphoria. Schenck felt just as he would if he had spent the night with the Biographer; if it had been her caresses which had forbidden sleep, rather than the slow task of writing (by which he hoped those caresses might be won). He tried to imagine (or rather, he observed himself trying to imagine) that it was a night spent with her which was the true cause of his condition. Rising from the table, and gathering up the papers which lay upon it, he tried to act as one whom luck has recently favoured. His gestures (the swing of an arm to arrange his hair, the stretching and arching of his back) were made not in the manner of an exhausted writer, but of a satisfied lover. In his mind, he observed himself comparing and differentiating these opposing possibilities. From his present sensations, how could he tell with certainty that it was toil to which he had sacrificed the night, and not love?

He went out quietly, careful not to make any sound

which might disturb Frau Luppen, whose gentle snores could be heard singing from her bedroom. He walked through empty streets until he arrived at his place of work (long before anyone else), then found himself sitting at his desk eating a bread-roll he had left the previous day. The food in his mouth had no taste, only a rough dry texture. He longed for his colleagues to appear, and for the day to propel itself forward into those comfortably mundane regions with which he was acquainted. And yet he also enjoyed this privilege of being alone and nobly bereft of sleep; of feeling with every movement the effort of volition and concentration, of feeling within himself the process (normally ignored) of living, of being alive — a sensation which, in the rush of the day, it is so easy to overlook. By being aware of his lack of sleep, he was made aware of what it feels like to be awake; he understood the complexity, the richness of simple acts which would otherwise be no more than reflexes. And if he had lain with the Biographer, and now felt as sleepless as this, how much greater would be his elation? If he had drunk his fill of physical love, lying and twisting in her arms throughout the night, would he now have found himself imagining some other kind of satisfaction, in which the unrested body may make a subtly different kind of protest?

Eventually they began to appear, those other workers who greeted their colleague with surprise and admiration, or with knowing looks whose silent interrogations the Cartographer chose to answer as ambiguously as possible. Now he could begin the difficult task of getting through his day's work without falling asleep over it. In his satchel all the while, the manuscript lay waiting, which had cost him his rest.

At the first available opportunity, he went upstairs to deliver it. There was the Biographer again, still labouring over the life of the Count. He had thought about her so much during the previous night, and had made such an effort to recreate her in his mind, that she seemed to him to be almost unrecognizable, now that he could see her again. His dreams had taken root upon a single image, a single moment during which he had seen her bowed head. This picture had been only imperfectly preserved, and the face he had raised and kissed in his mind was one of his own design; an interpretation of that bowed head and its many implications. The woman whom he now saw, the real woman, fitted only approximately into his reconstructions, so that he was able to approach her almost casually, as if she were a stranger.

He presented the hand-written pages to her, explaining that he had borrowed them from a copyist in the Literature Division. He could not vouch for the accuracy of the account, but would continue to search for more information. The Biographer expressed her thanks, and said that she would need a little while to study the text.

'Shall I come back later?' he asked.

'I might not have had time to read it all by then. Why don't we meet this evening?'

These words stunned the Cartographer before they could delight. Not only was the plan which he had formed working perfectly, but it now seemed that the Biographer was willing to take the initiative, in a manner so assertive as to be almost intimidating. The story whose composition had cost him a night's sleep was no more than an excuse, enabling the two of them to arrive at this moment of negotiation. And now they had become co-conspirators, each involved in a plot of their own joint making, though its ramifications were still deliciously uncertain.

She would meet him at the main entrance at the end of the day. Then she returned to the papers before her, and he left.

He was working on a map of the drains and sewers of Rreinnstadt. In the interlocking web of lines, wrapping and curling like a nest of snakes, he imagined he saw two writhing figures, bathed in perspiration. But now the day stretched before him like the coils of a great indolent reptile; the hours magnified by his impatience and desire to know what fate might await him that night.

Meanwhile there was still other work to be done. What about Pfitz? Once more, Schenck brought out the map on which he had discovered him. He examined the room in the tavern, where the Count lay in his bed. The figure of Pfitz, he now could see, had already been subjected to some correction. And the pencilled lettering of his name was in a different hand from the rest of the map. Who had put him there? Perhaps Balthus had taken the answer with him to the grave.

Schenck examined the paper minutely. He held the page up to the light, looked at the lines from the reverse side, through the thickness of the sheet. He searched for some meaning in the poorly drawn symbol; an irregular patch suggesting perhaps a blanket beneath which Pfitz lay sleeping. And Schenck could see now that beside this mark there were the indentations of letters which had been erased. He spelled them out one by one, until he formed a word. *Spontini.*

So here was another character in the Count's story. Another fragment which Schenck had excavated, and which he would somehow have to fit into a picture which would eventually include his joyful union with the Biographer.

He tried the General Catalogue again, and this time the effort was rewarded. There was an entry for Spontini; it was the name of a writer. There were no further details, but Schenck had what he needed. Now he could go to the Literature Division to find out more.

This was situated in another building, and it was not a place which Schenck had ever previously considered visiting. In the great circular Reading Room, he was greeted by the awesome sight of the densely loaded shelves, towering high and extending in every direction.

At the desk, an Attendant sat hunched over a large book. Schenck approached quietly, hesitating to speak for fear of interrupting his reading. Suddenly the Attendant gave a chuckle, and the raising of his head enabled him to notice the visitor.

'Good afternoon to you,' the Attendant said, then felt obliged to comment on the volume before him by way of explanation for his outburst. 'Rimmler's next book. One of Rreinnstadt's finest authors. So fresh.'

He said this in a manner which was almost conspiratorial, as if he expected Schenck to know all about Rimmler, though in fact he had never heard of him.

'His *next* book?'

'Still unfinished. But it's going to be one of his best, I can tell.' And then he lowered his head once more, as if the presence of the Cartographer were no more than a brief interruption. He was studying the lines of what Schenck now could see to be pages of neatly written manuscript; the text ending halfway down one of the sheets. The Attendant was contemplating the blank part with great concentration.

'Of course!' he said at last, then took up his pen and began to write. 'This Rimmler,' he muttered; 'you never know what he'll come up with next.'

'But you're writing the book yourself.'

The Attendant looked up once more, reminded again of the inconvenient presence, and apparently irritated by such impudence.

'What of it?' he said.

'Is the book by Rimmler, or by you?'

The Attendant's expression was one of amazement at this demonstration of naivety.

'You clearly don't understand very much about the activities of the Literature Division. The work on which you see me engaged is one of my duties as part of the Authorship Committee. Rimmler's novels are produced by a team of five people, acting in co-operation. I am one member of that team. Everything we know about Rimmler himself comes from the Biography Section. We know, for example, that he will produce ten novels before his untimely death. This one is only his second – still in his youthful style. One of my colleagues, though, is currently researching the final works; there's no need for chronology, you see, as long as it all gets done . . .'

His irritation at being interrupted in his work was being soothed by the balm of discussing it.

'But how can you be surprised by something you've already written?'

'The words may be my own, but once put into the mouth of Rimmler, they take on a character which is wholly new. I myself can lay claim to no particularly great talent, but Rimmler is clearly a genius. I can't wait to see the finished book. None of us has the slightest idea how it will turn out.'

The Attendant was becoming more expansive now, but Schenck didn't wish to know anything more concerning Rimmler.

'I want to ask you about a writer called Spontini. Have any of his books been written yet?'

'The name doesn't sound familiar. I suppose it would be a job for the Italian Office, and they've been having all sorts of problems lately – they're so far behind schedule. You know, Carlo Montana is supposed to produce an Encyclopaedia in fifteen volumes, and his Committee still haven't got beyond Batavia. And as for fiction ... hopeless!'

'Are there many Italian writers in Rreinnstadt?'

'None at all, as far as I know. But there are plenty of books by them. You people don't realize what a great task it is – designing a building is nothing, compared with having to write all the books which would sit on one shelf inside it.'

'How do I find Spontini?'

'Have you tried the Index of Authors?'

'Where can I find that?'

'Haven't you bothered to consult the Index of Indices? It'll tell you there.'

'And I suppose I have to look up another Index in order to find the Index of Indices?'

'You could always try the Index of Indices Which Don't Include Themselves. You know, I do wish that members of the public would show a little more initiative before coming here and asking for help. I am trying to write a book, after all.'

Then the Attendant relented somewhat, no doubt savouring the opportunity to appear indispensable. 'Alright then, let's look the fellow up.' He began to leaf through the cards in one of the drawers beside him, and soon came up with something. 'Spontini. One incomplete work. Died insane. I suppose you want me to find his book for you now?'

'Does your record say any more about his life?'

'No, you'd have to try upstairs. But let me get that book.'

When the Attendant returned he handed a slim volume to the Cartographer. *The Aphorisms of Vincenzo Spontini.* Then the Attendant buried himself once more in his work.

The Cartographer took Spontini's book, and went back to the Cartography Office. Perhaps this was what Pfitz was reading as he lay on the floor, unable to sleep on its hard surface. Balthus might have entered the name of the Author by mistake, instead of its Reader. Although it seemed now that the hand which wrote the name of Pfitz may not be that of the late Balthus, after all.

So many questions – though already the mysterious Pfitz was becoming irrelevant. He would meet the Biographer in just a few hours – what further need did he have of the Count and his servant? They would discuss the manuscript he had given her; they would debate earnestly, ruminate and put forward conjecture and hypothesis; he would slip his arm around her (at an appropriate moment). Then Pfitz and the Count would disappear, Spontini would evaporate and there would be nothing left except a cloud of pleasure; an ecstatic meeting of her soft skin with his.

The hours elapsed so slowly, and Schenck's tiredness made the wait even more unpleasant, but at last the time came when he could leave. He put Spontini's book in his satchel – he might read it later on, though the evening promised more interesting distractions for him.

He reached the main entrance at the earliest possible

moment, before anyone else had begun to leave the building. He was determined not to allow any room for the possibility that he should miss her.

He waited there for more than an hour. He counted the bars on the gate, and the cobblestones on the road beside him. He compared the moss on one of the more shaded walls with that on an exposed face. He recited the verses of a dozen songs, and composed a few more besides. When the first of his fellow workers had begun to leave, he had stood proudly, hoping that they would notice he was waiting for someone. He had caught the eye of the women as they left, and tried to read in their expressions some recognition of his good fortune, perhaps even a hint of envy. Then, as their numbers thinned, he had gradually felt more and more awkward; turning his head away when he saw someone he recognized. At first, he had suffered only irritation at the Biographer's delay, but this irritation eventually swelled into something far more painful. He had crossed a boundary, difficult to recognize but nevertheless very real, between the initial period when he expected her at any moment, and the later one, during which he constantly asked himself how much longer he would wait before giving up and going home. He set himself targets, which he measured by the chimes of the church clock. If she did not arrive before the next quarter-hour, he would leave. She did not arrive. He stayed.

A passing dog took pity on him. It was a big black-and-white thing, and looked mournfully at him, clearly understanding what it means to be abandoned, to be ignored, to be tossed aside by the world. The dog sniffed his hand, then walked on.

Schenck went back inside to look for her. The door to the Biography Division was locked. He looked for a porter – perhaps she had been locked in the building? The porter threw him out.

And so he began to make his way home. It was already dark, and he did not pay any attention to his surroundings as he walked. He did not notice the figure who must, at some point, have decided to follow him along the lanes and into the darkness of a narrow alley in which there were no other people; a long stretch between two high and featureless walls. Schenck might have heard the footsteps behind him, but if he did he ignored them. And then he felt an arm encircling him from behind, pulling his head backwards.

He thought he might be strangled. One arm was pulling tight at his neck, while the other was held fast across his body to prevent him from struggling. It occurred to him that this might be the moment of his death. The attacker was tugging at the Cartographer's satchel, trying to free it from his grip.

A passer-by happened to appear now at the other end of the alley, walking past the entrance and pausing only slightly to notice the scene. This was the piece of good fortune by which the Cartographer was saved. His assailant immediately ran off, leaving his victim coughing and gasping for air. When Schenck reached the end of the alley, the passer-by had disappeared.

Fear, humiliation and wretchedness swept over him in a wave of blackness. He fainted.

When he regained consciousness he was lying, fully clothed, on a bed which was very large and very soft. Flussi was licking his hand.

'Stop it darling. Look, you've woken him now.'

Frau Luppen sat at the bedside. He didn't recognize this room, in which everything seemed to be pink. It must be Frau Luppen's own.

'Don't try to move. You gave your head a hard knock when you fell.'

'How did I get here?'

'A pair of chimney sweeps recognized you and brought you home. Left soot on the rug, as well. But what were you doing falling down like that in the street? You can't be eating enough. Or was it a fight? Don't tell me you've become a duellist over some young woman.'

Frau Luppen's conception of the world was based on the romantic novels which she found so entertaining.

'I don't remember what happened.' This was not completely true, but Schenck felt strangely ashamed of the attack – which he was now beginning to recall – as if it revealed some weakness in him.

'I thought it best to put you here, rather than have those fellows try and take you upstairs. Such dirty shoes! But now that you're awake, do you want some soup?'

Schenck told her that he wasn't hungry, and that really he felt well enough to get up and go to his room, but as soon as he tried to move, his head ached with renewed force. Frau Luppen told him that she had already sent for a doctor, which only made him feel even worse.

Schenck had undressed and got into bed by the time the doctor arrived. The doctor tried some apricot brandy, and complimented Frau Luppen on her comely appearance, then told her that the patient would be fine after a day in bed and to contact him again if there were any problems. Then he charged her ten crowns and wished her good evening. Schenck said he'd pay her back.

'Just rest yourself.'

'And where will you sleep tonight?'

Frau Luppen giggled. Her bed was in another room. If he needed anything, he only had to call out to her.

He slept well, despite the snores of his landlady. Next morning she brought him toast and honey, and sat by the bed watching him eat it, as if afraid that he might miss a crumb. He was moved by her kindness, though her fussing irritated him. He simply wanted to be left alone.

He tried to get up, but realized that the doctor was right; he should spend the day in bed. To lose a day's wages was bad enough (not to mention the doctor's fee), but what pained him far more was that he would not be able to see the Biographer, so as to discover what had happened to her. Would she perhaps look for him, and worry that he was not at work? This hope sustained him.

The day was long and tedious. Frau Luppen provided relief of a sort, with her anecdotes and advice, and her endless expressions of concern each time she came into the room to attend to him. Then when he was left alone to rest he stared at the cracks of light from the shuttered window, and thought of the bright, living world outside which was somehow running like water through his fingers. The only possibility of diversion was the book which lay in his satchel beside the bed; the *Aphorisms* of Vincenzo Spontini. He brought it out, and began to read.

Chapter Six

Spires, turrets, gargoyles; the twisting decoration of a column, the tracery of a window. In the cathedral, I find myself in a nest of vipers; a labyrinth of poisoned stone encircles me, enlacing my thoughts. I am in the interior of a cold body, whose last fading sigh continues to resonate. This would have been the right place to do it; after the mass had ended, before she could leave, and while the vigilance of the others would still have been lowered. The path of a blade through space: the gleaming arc of a circle, its radius equal to the length of one arm, defined by a dream, by impossible motion. A dream which would have begun and ended in this place, in the swift impossible motion of a blade.

What does it feel like, to have these thoughts? As I read them, I try to recall the emotions with which I wrote them. Yet the task is so difficult that I begin to wonder whether they are the words of someone else, and have simply been left for me here in my cell, as another way of torturing me.

Once again, the memory of that great book, laid open in the observatory. The secrets of the universe transcribed by the hand of my astrologer into figures on a page – the secrets of the past, and of the future also. Everything is governed by the motion of those spheres which surround us. Our actions, our desires; the motion of a robed figure across a church, the raising and lowering of an arm: everything is controlled by the indifferent movement of the spheres.

It was I who walked across the church; I feel sure of this. But does a false memory feel any different from a genuine one? It may have been another person, another Prince, who walked in that church – who walks there still. Perhaps I am inventing these words: not even reading them, but writing them with my imagination. I believe the words lie before me, but the paper and the cell itself may be another of their tricks, sent to deceive me.

He compiled my horoscope, showed me how his calculations converged on my own fate, and that of my subjects. Wealth, fame, glory — all no more in fact than the fortuitous consequence of an equation. Beauty also, and grace; the softness of skin, the swaying of a limb, all the result of an uncaring mechanism which lies beyond us; above us. The beating of a heart, its quickening. Its unfaithfulness. He showed me the calculations; those rows and columns of irrefutable data. This would have been the place, I'm sure of it.

Are my thoughts the consequence of another of his equations? It occurs to me that he may be thinking of me; these words might be a thought in his head, not in mine. My words might be no more than a path traced out by the indifferent course of the stars.

Again I remember the observatory; the peace and mysterious stillness of that room at the top of the tower. In daytime it seemed like a place asleep; the astrologer sitting over the charts and figures spread upon a table, stroking his long grey wizard's beard with unwashed fingers. The room smelled of pigeons, and of his feet. A clock ticking somewhere — several clocks, and instruments all around; sextants, globes, compasses. Another universe, and full of dust.

He pointed at an entry on the chart he had made; my wife's horoscope. The intention was now proved, and the predisposition. All that remained was to calculate where and when, and with whom. He pointed with long unwashed fingers at the mathematical demonstration of my worst fears. Her heart, I now realized, was another wandering star, pulled away by an irresistible force of attraction. I would follow the path of that beating star, that red flickering globe of inconstancy.

I try to tell myself that none of this exists, and the thought is a comforting one. I am not the author of my actions, and need feel no remorse. I am instead a reader — one amongst many. The life which I imagined to be my own is simply a text provided for my diversion. The words which they have provided for me is the life of someone else; someone else's thoughts and memories.

The observatory provided a good place from which to watch

the streets below, as well as the heavens above. With the aid of the telescope, the contents of a window could be examined just as easily as the craters of the moon, or the phases of Venus. From the room at the top of the tower, I could begin my observations of the city beneath me, that galaxy of intrigue and deceit. I could begin to gather my data, formulate my theories. It was draughty up there, with only the occasional stray pigeon for company. The sound of the wind, and the flapping of their wings against the roof. A loose feather wafting and floating – I watched one once; grey and white, and fluttering down towards the city. My own life, and my crimes – real or imagined – no more than a feather on the breath of the Gods.

It almost feels as if I wrote these words myself, as if they do not come from that other one (the darker one). I see him still, even in my cell; at night, sometimes, amongst the flickering shadows when the candle sputters out its final yellow stains of light. It almost feels as if it was I who thought those words, as if it were I myself who held an entire kingdom in being through no more than the power of belief. I see him now, that other one; myself, sitting high in the observatory. I read the words he wrote for me.

Each day, I would look down upon the city. The telescope was difficult to control, but with time I mastered it. I could steer it towards the objects and places which I sought – that door from which she would appear (the time marked patiently by the clock which ticked beside me); then turn to her left – my right – and walk some distance to another door, which would be opened for her. All quite innocent. And the room upstairs, whose tiny window I could, with the aid of the telescope, unpick like a miniature embroidery. Those specks and pearls of light pulled each from the other – the square window made wider, larger. And the contents of the room laid bare, like the entrails of a captured fox. I could almost touch them, they seemed so close. Like two dolls, in a toy house. My own wife, my own servant.

Two insignificant planets, whirling through an uncaring universe. Motes of dust floating through empty darkness, like the great empty hollow of a church, dimly lit (the candles almost burnt out) –

a solitary wretch, an existence defined only by the motion of a robed figure.

I am there once more. I see him: my own robed figure. I am not the author of my actions. The astrologer, he explained it all to me. We are no more than a pattern of stars, our lives a kind of constellation, cold and pure, and floating in infinite darkness. This cell in which I imagine myself to be sitting is an illusion. Even the words I write – or think I write – are another illusion, sent by them into my mind, in order to trick me.

Astrologos: the language of the stars. The cosmos might then be some kind of great book, stars and planets are its words; the motion of a comet, a statement whose meaning must be discerned. That observatory, high in the tower, was the place from which one could try and read the heavens, or else look downwards, and seek to read the workings of a wayward heart.

And the church. Here was the place, and the moment. Now I have lost it, just as I lost her. Already she is escaping – her disc is receding, along the great arc of an indefinite orbit. In my mind I see her once more, as I have seen her so often before, through the unswerving scrutiny of the telescope – a distant object, flickering with cold beauty, and drawn away by forces which are beyond my comprehension. A fading star; my own fading life, and the breath of the living and of the departed. Drawn away now into darkness, and the infinite void.

Chapter Seven

Frau Luppen came in to see how he was feeling.

'What are you reading, Herr Schenck? I hope it isn't something lascivious. You mustn't get yourself too excited.' The quivering of her dimples suggested the threat of a giggle.

Schenck told her he was much better, and would try to get up later. In fact, it was boredom and frustration rather than returning health which made him long to get out of bed.

'How's your temperature?' Frau Luppen had placed her plump knuckles against his forehead. Her face expressed doubt, and indecision. Without any further comment or excuse, she now put her cheek where her hand had been.

It was like a great soft cushion of unfathomable depth. A stray ringlet tickled Schenck's ear, and he could smell her perfume, which suggested flowers and children's parties. A pink sort of smell. And in that terrifying moment of closeness, the great continent of her bosom hung low in front of his face. He had an ample view of those great double orbs, trussed and squashed, which spread before him like fields of blue-veined snow. He need only flex his hand, stretch a finger, and he would prod their softness.

Somewhere, far above him, it was as if the figure of the Biographer were looking down in contempt.

Frau Luppen retreated, turned and left without saying a word. But now Schenck was disturbed by visions of that great mass, unclothed and giggling, pink and smelling of soap, bath oils, lavender and gardenia. Might this vision be no more than his revenge for the Biographer's indifference? And yet it was also a vision which frightened him; a vision of ugliness and imperfection – a bordello scene whose tawdriness made his heart sink just as quickly as it had made other spirits rise within him. Even so, he could not resist the fascination of that hidden realm, vast and undiscovered, whose contours he knew only in outline.

He wanted to read more of Spontini's book, but found himself unable to concentrate. Again he resorted to vacant observation of the shuttered window, its cracks and fissures of light.

Some time later, Frau Luppen returned to announce that a visitor had arrived. Gruber came in. 'What a pair we are! First my arm, then your head. At this rate there won't be any cartographers left by the end of the week.'

His jollity seemed slightly forced. Schenck and Gruber were colleagues, not close friends.

Schenck made his enquiries out of politeness. 'How does your arm feel now?'

'Back to normal and ready for action.' Gruber gave another throaty laugh, and the way he looked at Frau Luppen made her leave the room.

Schenck longed to know if Gruber had seen the Biographer again. He wondered how he could find out about the two of them without raising the subject directly.

'How exactly did you hurt your arm?'

'Bloody carriage. Ran straight over me.'

'Was anyone else hurt?'

'What do you mean?'

'Was there anyone else around?'

Gruber shrugged, and Schenck guessed that his rival had been no more successful than Schenck himself.

'And how are you getting on with the redhead?' Gruber asked; 'You moved pretty quickly to get that map back from her.'

'It was needed by someone else.'

'Really? And who might that have been?'

Their conversation rested uneasily on the borderline between good-natured teasing, and vindictiveness. They tacitly agreed to change the subject, and the true reason for Gruber's visit became apparent. He needed some expert advice from Schenck for a forthcoming map of underground streams. Once they were both on neutral ground, talking about technicalities, they both became much warmer. Schenck happily suggested books and sources which his colleague should consult.

'Thank you, Schenck. And is there anything I can do for you? Anything you'd like me to bring you from work?'

Schenck could think of many things, but he did not want to send Gruber on any errand which would bring him into contact with the Biographer.

'I'd like some information about a writer called Spontini. Just out of curiosity – I came across the name on a map.'

Gruber laughed inanely, and without sincerity, as if suspecting Schenck of some ulterior motive. Nevertheless he agreed to find out what he could. He stood up and left to go back to his work.

After he had gone, Schenck tried to get out of bed, but when Frau Luppen heard him she came to make him lie down again. She sat on the edge of the bed, looking sternly at him.

'I'll bet it's a woman who's the cause of all this. Fainting fits and not eating your food. Ah! you poor young thing.'

She gave his arm a squeeze, then decided to check his temperature again, only this time it was the back of her hand which she used once more. Schenck stared up at the great shelf of bosom which projected above his face. He tried to imagine the effort of tying up her corsets, which she would have to make each morning.

'I'm sorry that I never had the privilege of meeting your husband,' he said.

Frau Luppen withdrew her hand from his forehead. 'Yes. He was a good man.' She remained on the edge of the bed, and seemed uneasy.

'You must miss him a great deal.'

'Of course.' She looked down at her hands, which rested now like a knotted pudding on her lap. 'Such a sudden loss. So unexpected.'

'How exactly . . .?'

Frau Luppen stood up. 'Let's not talk of such things, Herr Schenck. He has gone to a better place now.'

'Amen.'

She was on the point of turning to leave, waiting for Schenck to say something else. He remained silent.

'Yes,' she continued, 'I do miss him. And the nights . . .'

Tears stood ready at the edges of her eyes. He might leap up now from his bed and try to unlace that great taut framework of whalebone and chord, if it were not for the fact that his head still ached. She left.

The day dragged itself into evening. Gruber called again. He came in and handed Schenck an envelope.

'This was on your desk. Don't know who it's from.'

The Biographer! Schenck longed to tear open the envelope, but instead he slid it beneath his pillow, for subsequent private study. Gruber also presented a sheet of paper.

'I copied this out for you. It's about that Spontini fellow – a queer sort if you ask me. Why do you want to know about him anyway? You're not thinking of moving up to Biography are you?'

Schenck ignored this, and took the paper. He thanked Gruber, and said that he was rather tired now, and had better sleep. Gruber nodded politely, expressed his wishes for Schenck's recovery in a conventional formula, and left.

The page was a biographical summary of Vincenzo Spontini. It gave dates and places, names of parents and so on, and concluded with a brief account of his work:

Spontini began the Aphorisms shortly before the onset of the illness which deprived him of his reason. Initially the book was conceived as a reworking of the story of the seventeenth century Prince Rudolphus, who murdered his wife on the advice of his astrologer, suspecting her of having had illicit relations with a servant. However, the deterioration in Spontini's health quickly led to a change in direction, so that the book gradually took on the character of an autobiography. The collective title 'Aphorisms' was given by a later editor to the disordered fragments which Spontini had produced by the time of his death.

The nature of Spontini's insanity was such that he became overwhelmed by the delusion, first of all, that he was in fact a character in his own book, rather than its author. He saw himself variously as the Prince and as the accused servant, and then imagined a series of authors struggling to gain control of his soul. Finally, he was led to believe that he did not exist at all, except in the minds of others. The crisis culminated in the murder of his own wife, whom he stabbed to death, convinced of her unfaithfulness. He was arrested soon afterwards, his only comment being: 'This is where the story ends.' He was incarcerated in an asylum, where he continued to work on what was to become the Aphorisms until his death eighteen months later. For further details, see the complete Biography.

What was Pfitz doing with Spontini's book? Was this really the reason why the writer's name had been erased from the Count's room? This third character in the Count's unfolding story was a disturbing one. Tomorrow, he would try to find out more.

Now Schenck drew the envelope out from beneath his pillow. He searched in vain for some fragrance which would evoke the Biographer's skin. He hoped for some explanation for her absence the previous night, but the message inside did not provide it. *Bring more of Pfitz*. That was all. No thanks, no apology.

Schenck got up out of bed and dressed himself. He had lost a whole day to his infirmity, but his head no longer ached, and he had had enough of being an invalid. He told Frau Luppen that he would go upstairs to his room. She pleaded with him to be careful in case he should faint again, but to no avail. The sickness he felt had nothing to do with any physical injury.

In his room, he sat down once more at the little table by the window. The inkwell and paper were still in place. He had to bring her more. And so he began to write the next part of Pfitz's story.

64

Chapter Eight

COUNT: What was your father the glazier like?

PFITZ: Let me tell you my earliest memory of him. He is counting coins at his bench on the other side of the room. My mother is sewing. Then he turns from his work, grabs her round the waist and starts kissing her.

COUNT: What a shameful thing to remember!

PFITZ: I can't help it. Now he pulls her onto the bed and has his way with her, before my own eyes.

COUNT: I can't believe that at all — I can't believe that they would do such a thing right in front of their own child, or that you could possibly remember it. You must have dreamed it up — a false memory brought about through drink.

PFITZ: Not at all, sir. It truly happened before my eyes, and I watched what was going on and thought what a funny sight it was. I don't know exactly how I thought it, since I didn't yet know then how to speak — I possibly didn't even know how to laugh, in which case I don't know how I could imagine a thing to be funny; but in any case, I remember seeing my parents making love.

COUNT: That's quite absurd. I tell you, you imagined the entire thing. You probably dreamed it all last night after you went to bed drunk in that revolting tavern where we were forced to stay, and now you think the dream that's still in your head is a memory. You've never told me this story before, you know.

PFITZ: Just because I never told it sooner doesn't mean it didn't happen, sir. It's taken me a lifetime to acquire all the stories that are in my head, and it would take more than a lifetime to tell them. But I can be sure that the memory is genuine, because as I watched my father's backside bob up and down, I noticed a very unusual scar upon it.

COUNT: I'm not sure I want to know about your father's private regions . . .

PFITZ: And some years later I chanced to ask him about it. I don't know how the subject came up, but I said to him (I was still a boy, mind): father, how did you get that mark on your behind? He went red as a cherry and I thought he was going to get angry, but I think it was actually a blush of shame and surprise. He asked me how I knew, and I lied and said that I'd seen him once get up out of his tub. So he said he'd tell me the story.

Then Pfitz told his master how, many years earlier, his father fought at the battle of Brunnewald. His father (who was called Hans) was hardly more than a boy himself – fifteen or sixteen years old maybe –, and he was enlisted as a drummer. The regiment had to march for two days, in driving rain, with not a scrap to eat save whatever they could scavenge from the land. They arrived at a small hamlet, and decided to make camp. There were only a couple of farms with a few sheds and barns, and the Colonel said that they would shelter in these. Taking pity on young Hans, who was shivering and hungry, he took him to find food at one of the farmhouses.

The Colonel banged on the door until eventually a pretty young girl opened it, who could hardly refuse entry to the two strangers outside. The girl was called Lise, and she lived with an ancient woman who had adopted her when Lise was abandoned as a baby – left for dead in the turnip field (or so she said). The Colonel and Hans came in and met the old woman, who was deaf and almost blind as well, and Lise put out two bowls of soup for them. They ate heartily, and then the Colonel said it was late and they must retire. Lise suggested a room behind the kitchen where the two of them could billet, but the Colonel said that a man of his position couldn't possibly do without a proper bed and a room of his own. So he was given a bed upstairs, while Hans had to make do with the stone floor of the scullery. Of course, part of the Colonel's plan was to be nearer to Lise, who was a very charming girl, and to be able to enact his plan without interference.

COUNT: I detect, as usual, a scurrilous motive behind your story; a story which is certainly false. What you mean to do is dress up the events of last night so as to mock me.

PFITZ: Not at all, sir. My story has got nothing whatsoever to do with the tavern where we slept last night, or that pretty girl whom you found so interesting. The coincidence, like everything else in this world, is completely accidental.

COUNT: Is it also an accident, then, that the girl in your story should share the name of the one last night?

PFITZ: In truth, sir, I have borrowed the name, since I can't remember exactly which one my father used when he told me the story. In fact, I believe that on the various occasions he recounted it, the girl's name was either Lise, or Gretchen, or Magdalena . . .

COUNT: Which only goes to prove that if you are not a liar then your father was.

PFITZ: Forgive me sir, but that is a very grave accusation to make. If my father changed a few minor details in retelling the story, it was only so as to hold the interest of his audience, since there is surely no point in telling exactly the same tale twice.

COUNT: There is if you care about the difference between fact and fiction.

PFITZ: In my experience, sir, there is no difference whatsoever. Whether the events I tell you about really occurred, or whether we ourselves are no more than fictions in some greater story, are questions too subtle for me to contemplate.

COUNT: Don't try to baffle me with your philosophizing. I believe that you intend to tell me a story about a Count, or a Colonel, who spends the night in a room next door to a girl called Lise . . .

PFITZ: Then during the night that Count or Colonel decides to get out of bed . . .

67

COUNT: To relieve himself . . .

PFITZ: And finds himself returning to the wrong bedroom? You are quite wrong, sir. This was not the story in which my father found himself all those years ago, and it would be a miraculous coincidence had he done so.

Then Pfitz continued, and told how his father, Hans, fell asleep as soon as he lay down on the hard floor, so exhausted was he from the day's long march. The next thing he knew was a terrific crash which brought him awake in terror. The whole house seemed to have been shaken and lit up for an instant. They were firing the cannons outside – a small platoon of enemy soldiers had found the camp and decided to attack; they didn't seem to know that the battle wasn't due to start for another day and a half, over at Brunnewald. There weren't many of them, but they had managed to throw the regiment into total confusion, having caught them most unfairly in their sleep, in clear contravention of international law. Soon, one of the barns was ablaze and men were running everywhere in panic, convinced that an entire army had advanced upon them. Hans stayed shivering in the scullery, watching the awful scene outside. The men, in their confusion, were firing on their own companions – which only added to the hopeless turmoil. In the end, the regiment managed to rout itself utterly – a self inflicted defeat which sent every soldier running out into the woods for safety, never to be seen again.

Eventually it was over – Hans's first sight of conflict had been a most unsettling one. He sat down again on the cold floor. It had lasted less than half an hour, and now all that remained was a bitter smell and a most eerie silence. Of the Colonel, there had been no sign. Hans decided to go and look for him. He went to the foot of the stairs, and waited in case he might hear something – but there was not a sound. And so, in the darkness, he began to make his way up, one slow step at a time. For all he knew, that terrible foe who had so thoroughly vanquished his regiment could already have won possession of this very farmhouse – its every room and dark recess giving shelter to a murderous enemy soldier.

Hans reached the top of the stairs, and saw three doors on the landing. He crept up to the first, listened at it, then gently pushed it open. Inside, there was nothing but an empty bed, the covers cast aside. The Colonel's coat lay neatly folded on a chair. Then the second door – again Hans waited, his ear pressed against the thick wood. From within, only the faintest sound – a kind of rhythmic rasping and wheezing, like a gate in a breeze, as it swings back and forth. He turned the handle, and looked inside to see his ancient hostess, fast asleep on her back. This left the third and final door. Hans went towards it with fear and trepidation. The Colonel and Lise were unaccounted for – if they had survived, then they were behind this door. But if the enemy had intruded while he lay hidden in the scullery, then what scene might await him?

COUNT: And you're trying to tell me that this has nothing whatsoever to do with the events of last night? The Colonel has left his room and gone to Lise's. What do you propose to tell me next? That Lise had already left and gone somewhere else?

PFITZ: Was that how it happened last night?

COUNT: You know perfectly well how it all happened last night. I left my bed to relieve myself . . .

PFITZ: There was no chamber pot?

COUNT: None. A most dreadful omission, and quite in keeping with the general condition of that wretched tavern. So I went wandering around to see if I could find a privy.

PFITZ: And found none, so you decided to return to your room.

COUNT: Indeed, just as I told you.

PFITZ: Were you not still eager to relieve yourself?

COUNT: The urge had subsided, and I wanted only to go back to sleep. But in the darkness and in my confusion,

69

unfamiliar as I was with the arrangement of rooms . . .

PFITZ: You found yourself in the wrong one, and did not realize until you had got into bed that someone lay beside you. An easy mistake, and quite understandable. But let me carry on with my father's story.

Hans stood outside the last door. He paused and listened, but from within that room there came no sound at all. At last, Hans decided to open the door. Gently, he turned the handle until he felt the latch come free, and then – very slowly – he pushed the door open. As he looked round it, and into the room, he saw revealed behind its retreating panel the awful sight of the Colonel, lying dead on the floor, his own sword still embedded deeply in his chest. On the edge of her bed, Lise was sitting silently, her hands and shift stained with blood. There was no need for explanation – it was clear what had happened. In defending herself from his advances, Lise had had to resort to using his own sword against him.

COUNT: Do you mean now to kill me in your stories! What treachery is this?

PFITZ: Master, this is not your story; it is my father's. Had it been your own story, then everything would have gone rather differently. When Hans opened the door, what would you expect to see inside? The Colonel embracing Lise? Or would you have preferred to see the Colonel alone and soundly sleeping, Lise having already left her bed and gone sleepwalking? Or would you expect to see Lise alone, while the Colonel, still wandering about and needing to relieve himself, had ventured outside and been caught up in the ensuing battle, in which he had acquitted himself most honourably?

COUNT: Any of these stories would be preferable to the sad death of the Colonel.

PFITZ: But none of them would be my father's story. So let me tell you the rest of it.

There was an urgent knocking at the door below, which

70

roused both Hans and Lise from their dazed shock as they stared at the bloody corpse of the Colonel. Now voices were calling from outside in an unknown language. It was the enemy! Hans closed the bedroom door behind him and with the sudden strength and presence of mind which only terror can inspire, he dragged the body of the Colonel into place as a barricade which might hinder the entry of the enemy into the room where he and Lise could now only pray for survival. Downstairs, the lock was being forced. Noises now, as things were knocked over and broken, valuables searched for. The enemy soldiers were almost certainly drunk, and jubilant at their easy and unexpected victory. There was a rapid thudding, as heavy boots came up the stairs.

The old woman in the other room was beyond help; for Hans and Lise there was only one place to hide now, and this was under the bed. It was a heavy thing, with a wooden frame and ropes tied across to support the horse-hair mattress, but there was just enough room for the two of them to crawl underneath, Hans lying almost on top of Lise since the bed was too narrow for them to fit side by side. They heard the door being pushed, the rattling of the handle – the man outside was shouting to his friends, who were running to join him. Several of them now pushing at the door, which was sliding open as the Colonel's lifeless frame was pushed aside. And then their laughter at their discovery – had they been sober and had any sense, the enemy soldiers would have realized that this sorry figure behind a closed door necessarily implied the presence still of his murderer, unable to escape. But no such thought occurred to them – perhaps they concluded that he had fallen upon his own sword, or else they were too drunk to give the matter any reflection at all. They dragged the body downstairs, the Colonel's boots bumping on the steps with his last sad descent, and they took him out and left him lying on the ground. When they came back upstairs they dealt with the old woman – again the heart-rending sound of a corpse dragged away. Then, after this bloody work, it was time for them to sleep.

Two of them came back into Lise's room. All the while, she and Hans shared terrified breaths beneath the bed, their mouths almost touching; their rapid stifled panting made all the more painful by the mutual pressure of their adjacent chests. But when two drunken foreign soldiers heaved themselves onto the bed, then it really was almost too much to bear. The two underneath felt themselves suddenly crushed each into the other – their mouths and cheeks smeared into a painful congruence, their bodies moulded into agonizing symmetry. Only the uncrushable will to survive prevented them both crying out then against such suffering, but instead they remained silent, unable to move and barely able to breathe. After a few minutes, the heavy sighs above them turned into snores.

This might have been a time for escape, had movement been possible, but they were pinned there in a position as rigid as it was uncomfortable. Their only hope came in those moments when one or other of the soldiers above happened to roll in his sleep. This invariably provided welcome variety and relief, but at times it promised also the possibility of some freedom – the brief opportunity to flex a limb, or to vary the angle of the head.

Hours went by – long hours during which Hans and Lise remained trapped together beneath the bed. Eventually one of the soldiers was interrupted in his sleep by a fit of coughing. The pounding of his shaking body brought forth a whole new repertoire of discomfort for the two prisoners, but at the end of it he sat up for a moment to clear his throat, and the shifting of his weight enabled the two of them to disconnect their numb faces. Next, the soldier swivelled and put his feet on the floor, as if about to get up. The feet appeared on Hans's side – the lessening burden above his shoulder allowing him in turn to lift some of his weight from poor Lise, who was carefully sliding herself nearer to the outer edge of the bed – slightly less afraid now of being seen, since her own soldier had shown no sign of waking.

In that tiny prison beneath the bed, a frenetic process of

72

rearrangement was underway. By comparison with what had gone earlier, this minute seemed like a time of luxurious comfort – the two of them were stretching like sleepy cats. Now Lise was replacing Hans in the uppermost position, lying across his back, while he remained face down – each of them free now to breathe air which had not already been consumed by the other. It seemed like the sort of position in which sleep would be an easy pleasure – itches and irritations could be attended to, minor adjustments made, before settling down.

Then the soldier thudded back into his place, and suddenly that great double weight returned with all its force – except that now the two trapped souls were quite unprepared for it when it came. Lise had been reaching to scratch herself – her arm having stretched as far as it could. The crush had taken her completely unawares – her hand was lost, isolated; stranded in a region into which it should never have ventured. The arm was twisted uncomfortably, the fingers bent and pinned in place. And her fingernails were lodged very firmly in Hans's left buttock.

Once more, this should have been a time for a loud, heartfelt cry of pain. It should have been a time for immediate withdrawal, for sincere apology. But this was the most perilous moment of their young lives, and each knew that this most unfortunate contortion would have to remain static and preserved, like a fly in amber, until such a time as further movement up above would make rearrangement possible. That time, however, would not arrive before dawn. For many hours, her fingernails would remain pressed into their wounded bed of flesh, while the two captives lapsed into a drowsy sleep brought on by exhaustion so great that it conquered all fear.

Eventually the soldiers rose. They wasted no time in the humble cell which had given them shelter for the night; they roused their comrades, and after quickly collecting together (in accordance with international law) everything in the farmhouse which was edible, valuable or otherwise of interest, they all went out together into the morning air,

73

laughing and shouting as they rediscovered the bodies of the Colonel and the old woman.

As their voices receded, Lise and Hans dared at last to slide themselves out from under the bed. They stood up together, their emotions swaying between the tearful joy of survival, and sorrow at the terrible events that had taken place. At last they embraced.

By now, they had each come to know every contour, every fold and recess of their companion's body – but in a form which was compressed and painfully distorted. This new embrace, however, was that of two souls let free – and their bodies were now strangers to each other; mysterious and unfamiliar. Hans reached for his wounded rump, still smarting. Lise could now make her apology, and she offered to put something on the wound to help heal it. Hans resisted, out of modesty, but then Lise said that she too had suffered during the long night. Without the slightest shame, she raised her shift, still stained with the Colonel's blood, and Hans saw in the middle of her naked belly the livid bruise, in four blue sections, left by his own hand. He stared at his fingers and palm, and tried to compare their form with the mark he had made, through sustained and imperceptible pressure, on the white flesh of the girl. And then he pulled down his thin breeches, and tried to turn enough to see what she had done to him – a similar wound, more localised though, where her nails had pierced the inadequate protection of his clothing. A stinging curve, made from four smaller crescents of torn flesh. She would put milkweed and dog lettuce on it, to ease the pain – but the mark would never go. 'We each bear the imprint of the other,' she said; 'we are like twins now. You must go today and find your regiment, and you will never see me again, but I shall always carry this wound in memory of you, just as you will always remember me. You will never know any woman's body as well as the one you see before you, nor will you ever come as close to any woman's heart as you have come to mine.'

74

COUNT: But his regiment was lost, and the Colonel. How then did he reach the battle of Brunnewald?

PFITZ: He walked all day until he met up with another regiment, which took him as drummer boy and treated him as a hero for being the sole survivor of his unit.

COUNT: And what sort of a story was that for a father to tell his young son?

PFITZ: A very strange one, I grant you; but my father was a most unusual man. In any case, the story is open to some doubt – much later, when I was already grown up, my mother denied that my father was ever at the battle of Brunnewald, and on another occasion said that he had always borne an unusual mark as a result of sitting on a clothes-brush as a child. But parents are always lying to their children, and husbands to their wives. Who knows what truth there is in any of it? All I can say is that if my father had never lived to tell me it, then I would not have been born to listen.

COUNT: He must have been a very reckless parent, to tell such a strange story to his own son.

PFITZ: Would you prefer, then, to hear a different story? In which a certain gentleman rises from his bed in the middle of the night to relieve himself, and in his confusion returns to the wrong room?

COUNT: An honest mistake.

PFITZ: And gets into bed, not noticing that someone sleeps there already?

COUNT: It was late, and very dark . . .

PFITZ: So that when this person, who may or may not be his own servant, awakens later on he has to contend not only with a thumping hangover, but also with the sight of a man who may or may not be his own master snoring soundly beside him after failing to find the room of the serving girl he had been looking for?

– Was this what happened last night?

It is possible, but hard to be sure now. The Author was asleep at the time, and we have only the word of Pfitz and the Count to go on. Pfitz was drunk, the Count was tired, and it was very dark. We shall return an open verdict on the issue.

Chapter Nine

Next day, Schenck returned to work. He still felt unwell, but his desire to see the Biographer, and to escape the attentions of Frau Luppen, persuaded him to go and present himself at the Cartographical Office. He took Spontini's book with him in his satchel, along with his new manuscript, hoping to be able to show it to the Biographer at the earliest possible opportunity.

He still did not even know the name of this woman who had caused him so much effort. Sometimes when he thought of her, he heard Gruber's description: 'The Redhead'. But he also imagined all the various names by which she might be known. He said these names to himself, while he imagined her writing at her desk, in the hope that if he discovered her true name it would manifest itself somehow; attach itself to the mental image and proclaim its authenticity. For several hours during the previous evening, he had managed to convince himself that she was a Clara. The name had seemed to fit her like a well-cut bodice, nestling into her every curve. But now the word had dried and shrivelled, and fallen from her like a dead leaf. He was waiting for another possibility to take its place.

Although he had only been absent for a day, his desk was piled high with items waiting for his attention; maps which required checking or correcting, and messages and requests from other departments. Most of these tedious chores had been redirected to him by colleagues taking advantage of his unavailability to refuse. But amongst all these papers, there was no word from the Biographer. It occurred to him to write her a message, but he quickly saw the folly of this. She would realize from the handwriting that Pfitz was his own work, and not that of a copyist.

It was some time before he was able to leave his office, and go upstairs to the Biography Division. There he found her, busily writing, as usual. He hoped at least for some expression of apology when she saw him, but instead she greeted him civilly, making no mention of what had happened.

'I would have come to see you yesterday,' he said, 'but I had to stay at home.'

'Were you ill?'

Schenck wondered what to say. He still felt strangely embarrassed about the incident.

'I was attacked in the street.'

The Biographer's mask of calm fell at last. She looked genuinely concerned. And everyone else in the room had suddenly become interested as well. Schenck looked around, and one by one the heads lowered.

'Can we meet later, to talk? To discuss the manuscript. Look, I have another piece of it here.'

The Biographer took it, but she seemed somehow confused, bewildered, as if thinking of something else; as if going through the stages of a difficult calculation.

'Yes,' she said, 'very well.' And Schenck's heart rose. 'Meet me after work.'

'How can I be sure you'll turn up?'

The Biographer was not to be drawn. She spoke almost in a whisper. 'Come back here and you'll find me. Wait until all the others have gone.' Once more, Schenck saw inquisitive faces rise and sink around the room like ducks upon a lake. He hoped that everyone had heard this moment of triumph.

He went back downstairs. It would be another day in which his maps were little more than a diversion from the delightful thoughts which teased his imagination. Any resentment he had still held over his fruitless vigil two nights previously was now erased; the events of this evening would, he was sure, vindicate all his efforts.

His mind skipped restlessly from one thing to another. He was tracing the course of a thousand rivulets along the streets of Rreinnstadt, on a chart which showed an area of the city after a heavy rainstorm. Each stream had been carefully calculated, its cargo of soggy leaves assessed and considered. Would the drains be able to cope? This was the crucial question which had occupied some of the finest minds for weeks and months. But Schenck found now that he really didn't care. One of the streams became a doodle; it curled and snaked in a manner defying all the laws of fluid mechanics. When he saw what he was doing, he simply rubbed out the pencil mark and started again.

He thought about Pfitz, and Spontini. He considered going to consult the map yet again, but refrained. Gruber was in there, and he didn't want to get into conversation. Not yet. Tomorrow, perhaps; once there would be something to talk about, or hint at.

The biographical summary which Gruber had given Schenck intrigued him, and he wanted to find out more. It must have come from the Literature Division. This would be the next distraction, with which he could make the day slip by. When an opportunity arose, he got up and made his way out to pay it another visit.

The Attendant was still engrossed in Rimmler. He sat with the book held in one hand, and a pen in the other, ready to strike. It was like watching a heron catching fish. Complete silence, immobility, and then 'Of course!', and the Attendant's pen swooping down to add a sentence, correct a piece of grammar, improve a metaphor.

When he finally noticed Schenck, he showed no sign of recognition. Books were his world, not people.

'I came to ask about Spontini.'

The mention of an author's name set the Attendant's thoughts in motion. The name was familiar; he had seen it a couple of days ago, in the index. And he had signed a book out.

'Yes; I was the one who borrowed it.'

'Do you want to return it now?'

'No, I wanted to find out more about Spontini.' Schenck brought out the biographical summary which Gruber had written.

'Try upstairs.'

He already had, before coming here, but had found the office closed.

'I can't help you then.'

Schenck was irritated by his obstinacy. 'What about the names of the writers who worked on Spontini's book; could you tell me anything about that?'

'Not this department.'

If the Attendant was to be of any help at all, then Schenck would have to try a different approach. 'You see, I find it a little hard to understand exactly how you work in the Literature Division. Spontini would be produced by several writers . . .'

'Probably.'

'And he went mad and apparently turned his book into a sort of autobiography.'

'These things happen.'

'Is that how it would all have been planned? Would the biographers have decided on Spontini's madness first, then the writers would follow?'

The Attendant closed his book, after carefully marking the place. He motioned Schenck to sit down.

'Take Rimmler, for example. There are five of us working on him. First of all, he is created by Biography – that's where everyone starts. And at some point in his early life, it becomes clear that he will be called to a literary vocation (Rimmler was encouraged at school by an enlightened teacher of rhetoric). Then we're called in. So far, all that exists of Rimmler are some dates (his death being only provisional; a lot can happen once the Department of Pathology stick their noses in), and a few anecdotes here and there. There's no personality to speak of; no essence. Only once Rimmler becomes an author, can that emerge. He is what he writes.

'The five of us discuss a few general ideas. We know what sort of books Rimmler reads, his family background and so on. We agree on four things: a title, a setting, a style and a plot. Then we all go away and start writing. After a week, we compare what we've got. We chop it all up and stick it back together again (I joke of course; the process is really a very subtle one, requiring years of practice). We synthesize our separate texts into a single piece. What we come up with in this way is something totally new. No one of us in particular has produced the piece; it contains something of each of us, and yet something else as well. It is greater than the sum of its parts. And this extra ingredient which emerges is the personality of Rimmler. It's a magical process, difficult to explain, but it always happens. Already after a week, he's taken on a life of his own.

'Then we all go away again to do the next part. We know how the story begins, and we know who's writing it. We can begin to sound like Rimmler as we write; we try to impersonate him. Again we combine our efforts, moulding them into the correct shape. And so it goes on.

'As each new piece of the book is finished, we send it to Biography, so that they can have a fuller impression of the person about whom they are writing. In the story there is a love affair – could this be based on fact? All writing is to some extent autobiographical, after all. So the biographers do their research, and perhaps they find that Rimmler had an opportunity to form a liaison with a governess whom he used to meet each day in the park. Biography sends us the details; we'll use it again in his writing later on.'

'Fascinating,' said Schenck. 'But if you'll forgive me for saying so, it all sounds a little artificial. How can an original work of fiction, and even a personality, be produced by such a large group of people?'

'Are you sure that isn't how it all really happens? When I sit down to write Rimmler, how many voices do I hear within my own mind? Can you be sure that you yourself are really a single person, and not many within one body?'

'Very well, but what about Spontini? How might a writer go mad?'

'There are many kinds of madness. But perhaps the elements of which he was composed came into disagreement. There may have been tensions, conflicts. It happens.'

Schenck was trying to take in everything he had heard.

The whole process seemed so mysterious, so improbable. And yet this place was crammed full with its fruits; the unending shelves of completed books.

'One thing I still can't quite understand. If several people work to produce one Author, then how can they manage to arrive so often at a single personality? I would have thought it would be more usual for each writer to go in his own direction.'

'The averaging process helps, when work is edited and reassembled. But also you must remember that the thing which holds all of us together in the League of Writers (of which I am a Senior Associate, First Class), is a sense of common purpose. We are all working for Rreinnstadt, and for our Authors, not for personal fame or public applause. To disappear in our work; this is our goal. And when we are creating the personality of our Author, I should explain that there are some tricks of the trade which help things along. You learn these things over the years.'

'Such as?'

'Well first of all, you should always begin with the Reader. At a very early stage of composition, we reach an agreement on who the book is to be for. Every Author writes for a particular Reader – it may be an actual person, or a memory, or a fantasy, but this Reader is always there in his or her imagination. We think a book is good if it makes us feel that we ourselves are that particular Reader which the Author had in mind. Then the book 'speaks' to us. It's one of the tricks of the trade. So once we've agreed on our Reader, we aim our writing in that direction. First invent your Reader, then your Author will naturally emerge.'

'I wonder who Spontini's Reader might be?'

'I hope you are able to find out. They keep rather irregular hours upstairs, but I'm sure you'll get hold of them eventually.'

Then the Attendant returned to his work. Schenck felt a new respect, as he watched this fragment of Rimmler's personality go once more into action.

The Department of Authorship was still closed without explanation, and so Schenck went back to the Cartography Division. His swirling streams held no interest. He was thinking about Spontini, Pfitz, these intangible personalities. He still didn't know who Pfitz really was; the character about whom he had written was a pure invention. And yet he had already acquired his own life, his own personality. These fictitious people were as real to him as the Biographer, that woman who was also still a matter of speculation, of hypothesis.

He had no heart for his maps. He pulled Spontini's book out of his satchel, opened it at random, and began to read.

Chapter Ten

The small courtyard behind the Palace; an arcaded square of white marble, arches hooping evenly from one slender pillar to the next. A place in which all that I have learned comes naturally into focus. Material substance, I have been told, is no more than a kind of movement; a kind of transition. In the quiet stillness of the courtyard, I meditate upon this doctrine.

Once more I hear their voices. They wake me up, rouse me from my sleep. The cell is cold and damp, but I know this to be another of their deceptions. They have created me as their servant, and yet it is so easy to disobey them! A voice tells me: think of the courtyard. And so I think instead of something else, and their hold over me is broken.

Everything, it is claimed, is a kind of motion. Not only is it the case that all matter is in constant movement, but this matter itself consists of the motion of some higher substance. In other words, motion is prior to matter, and exists independently of it.

Always deception, trickery, invention. I feel hungry, and some food appears, pushed under the door of my cell. It is as if my hunger created the food. As an experiment, I try to simulate the feeling of hunger, so as to see whether the effect is repeated and more food appears. When it does not, I wonder whether my simulation was sufficiently accurate. How can I compare my impersonation with the actual sensation? My memory of hunger may be just as imperfect as my memory of all the other things which once existed for me beyond this cell.

In the centre of the courtyard, a fountain splashing coolly in the mid-day heat, while I would sit in the shade. A flame of water, bubbling and curling softly, constant not in shape but rather in form, and continually replenished by the water passing through it. How is it that the water can hold its shape, when always it is changing? And are we ourselves no more than an imperfectly rigid form, through which a higher substance flows endlessly? And is the courtyard, along with my memory of it, no more than some flickering flame of the imagination?

One can be mistaken in one's beliefs, but is it possible to be mistaken *about* one's beliefs? If a person believes himself to exist, then he cannot be mistaken. But if a person claims not to believe in his own existence, how are we to respond to this? Do we say he is a liar? Even though we tell him that his voice, and the expression of his thoughts, prove him to exist, still he claims to be an illusion. Is he wrong in imagining himself to have such a belief?

Think only now of the courtyard. Square, white, perfect. And the arches: semicircular. Like a harmonious chord of music, held fixed. Stationary, and yet moving (voices trembling, trying to hold a note. Air passing through white throats. The slow echo of a great church). Tomorrow, I console myself, will be as endless in its coming as the melting of a snowflake in a river. And my end will be as endless as those semicircles, hooping from pillar to pillar, in an eternal square. The world is no more than the brief passing of some higher substance through an infinite void.

The author of these words denies his existence. How are we to respond to this? He claims that his words (which, we try to convince him, come from his own living mind) are instead the work of others; that he is a fiction dreamed up by unknown people, with inscrutable motives.

In the courtyard, a damsel fly hovers about the fountain. Long red body, thin and fragile; and wings glistening, their rapid beating imperceptible to the slowness of my vision. Beyond the fountain and the insect, my eyes now focussing on the distant arcade; her figure, looking as she did when she stood beneath the great concave breasts of the church's vaulted roof. The only sound, the splashing of the fountain, and somewhere far off the chirrup of crickets. The only sound in my memory, the silent vision of her head raised, her open mouth trembling and the long note held, sustained as it rose and flowed from her white throat and out into the body of the church. Her white body, no more than the slipping of consciousness through a brief separation in the curtained void. A coincidence of images: the high vaults of the church (white); the arcaded courtyard (white); her body, laid bare before me. All white.

None of this can have happened. The Prince and his wife are fictions, this cell in which I imagine myself to be imprisoned is a fiction. Voices speak to me, telling me that none of this is real, that I am a character within the story of someone else, that I am a thought in the mind of someone else, that I am hollow, empty; that the words I speak are written by those others, sent to me by those others. Yet still I doubt this. And by trying not to think of the courtyard, I find myself thinking about it after all. Is it possible to make yourself not think of something?

Inanimate substance, or the passing of some higher spirit through the spaces which we occupied, she and myself. Her white throat, trembling as her voice rose in a single note, and echoed beneath the vaults of the church. And then her figure, framed in the arcade before me not long afterwards. These two moments were, in reality, a single moment. It was a different woman I now saw, and yet the same event. In the church, I saw the wife of my master. Beyond the fountain, I saw the shadow of a damsel fly.

If it is not possible to make oneself not think of something, then what is it that controls this aspect of the mind over which we have no power? Does the mind have another mind all of its own? I read the words which they send me, these thoughts which purport to be mine, and yet seem strange to me. Perhaps I can discover amongst the handwritten lines the true identity of their author. I think I see him, and yet his figure is vague and difficult to discern.

Beyond the shadow of a damsel fly, beyond the pale flickering of a fountain, beyond the distant chirruping of crickets, or the remembered trembling of a long held note; the movement of a figure (white); the averting of eyes, but then an irresistible raising once more of the face, the holding of gaze, the sustained note of vision, from across the courtyard in which I would often ponder the doctrine which my master once taught me, that all matter consists of an unending form of motion. She turns away, goes out through an arched door into darkness made more obscure by distance and the brilliant light of the sun (white). *I rise, and walk around the arcaded courtyard, to the place in which I saw her move.*

Tomorrow I shall be taken out to meet my death. And only then, at that final moment, shall I be able to be certain whether or not the words of my master are indeed true; whether I really am no more than a river through which events have flowed, and the world itself no more than a greater river, in which all streams intermingle. A great cold river of endless darkness.

The courtyard — think only of this. White, brilliant white in the sunshine. And beyond the fountain, in the shadow of a damsel fly, the fugitive figure of a woman, half glimpsed as she moves away from the periphery of my vision. Is it really in order to do her bidding that I now stand up, and make to walk around the courtyard towards the place from where she has hastily retreated? And on the other side, the door ajar. The door through which I pass into darkness, and softness.

Into soft darkness. The darkness of a curtained room. A soft curtained void of darkness.

Chapter Eleven

Schenck tried to imagine the separate voices which had come together to create Spontini's work; conflicting, discordant voices which in the end drove Spontini to despair. He consulted yet again the map which fascinated him; the one which showed the Count's room in the tavern. The name which had been erased was certainly that of Spontini. As if Pfitz had somehow replaced him; this poorly drawn smudge upon the floor, his own name pencilled so hastily that it was barely legible. The stories of Spontini and the Count came together somehow; their intersection a mystery which perhaps only a thorough investigation of the documents in the Biography Department would uncover.

Gruber saw him. 'You're very interested in that map lately.'

Schenck made up some excuse about a particular problem he was working on.

'When you found me that information on Spontini, where did you get it from?'

'Department of Authorship. I still don't understand what all this is about, Schenck.' There was a tone of nervousness in his voice. Did he still hope to win the Biographer?

'I told you; just a name I came across.' Schenck was already beginning to feel that he was becoming enmeshed in something; that he was a point on a map of great complexity, surrounded by signs whose meaning he could not fully fathom. He still had to discover the true identity of Pfitz, but could turn to no-one for help. Gruber was his rival, and must be excluded from everything involving the Biographer, while she too must not be allowed to discover the falsehood which he had perpetrated in fabricating the documents he had given her.

He went back again to those infernal rivers of muddy rainwater. They coloured his mind, seeped into his speculations and dampened his every thought. He longed to tear the chart he was making into a thousand pieces.

The hours went by, and the time for his assignation approached. People were leaving; on the stairs, he could hear the brisk descent of other biographers. He waited until there was no one left in his own office, then went upstairs.

She was still at her desk, the only person now in the great room. As soon as Schenck entered she turned round to look at him, startled by the sound.

'Only me.'

And now she stood up. It was the first time Schenck had seen her rise from her desk, and she was taller than he had imagined. He felt a great urge to hold her. He approached and spoke.

'I've been wanting to ask you . . .' he hesitated. 'What happened? When I waited for you before, why didn't you meet me?'

She averted her eyes, as if in shame. 'I can't explain now.'

'Then will you tell me your name?'

She looked at him again, and smiled as if at a child. 'My name is Estrella.'

This had not been on Schenck's list of possibilities, but now that he heard it, he realized that it fitted her perfectly. All those other names which had floated around his memory of her face, like hovering insects, suddenly flew away looking absurd and inappropriate. Why had he not guessed it sooner?

'Have you had time yet to read all of the manuscript I gave you?'

'Not quite. Did you say it came from the Literature Division?'

Schenck had to tread carefully. 'The copyist works in the Department of Anecdotes.'

'What's his name . . .?'

'And the manuscript is due to be reviewed by the Literature Division. But it might still end up in the Office of Unreliable Information.'

89

'Will you tell me who he is, this copyist?'

Schenck wondered what to say. The thought of lying to her filled him with dread, and yet there was no alternative. 'I can't tell you his name, Estrella. You see, he was acting without authorisation when he showed me the documents. I don't want him to get into trouble.'

'In that case, who is the Author of Pfitz, who are his writers?'

'Forgive me, but this also is something which it is better for you not to know.'

'That's a pity,' she said. She was beginning to tidy her desk in preparation for leaving. 'The style is very interesting.'

'You like it?'

'I feel it speaks to me, in a way I can't exactly describe.'

Schenck was filled with pride, but tried not to show it. 'A good book is one which makes you feel as if it were written for you alone.'

'Ah how true,' said Estrella. 'I can see that you know how to appreciate literature.' She put her arm in his. 'Shall we go?'

It was a simple gesture, and yet to Schenck it was a message of such complexity that its explanation would fill volumes. They went out together, down the stairs and into the street, already dark and cold, and all the while Schenck held his companion close beside him, to such an extent that walking became at times rather awkward.

A full moon cast blue light over the buildings and the streets, transforming their daylight colours into a new set of hues belonging solely to the night. Schenck watched, from the corner of his eye, the figure who walked beside him; her pale skin, and lips which were no longer red. He could feel the warmth of her arm, though whenever he tried to draw her closer towards himself, she would pull gently away.

'Which way should we take?' he asked her.

'Take your usual route,' she replied. Was she inviting herself to his house? Occasionally, while they walked, she would look to the side, or over her shoulder, as if she feared they might be followed. When she had walked with Gruber, Schenck observed, she had shown no such signs of agitation. He longed to ask her for some explanation, but feared her answer.

Schenck raised once more the subject of Pfitz. 'The authenticity of the manuscript is still open to question. I'm continuing my researches. And there seems to be a connection with a writer called Spontini.' He felt a stiffening in her arm, as if in response. 'Have you heard of him?'

'No, never. What kind of connection?'

'I don't know yet. His name was erased from the map on which Pfitz appears.'

'Erased? By whom?'

'Presumably the map-maker, Balthus, though I'm afraid he is no longer with us.'

'How did he die?'

'I've no idea. Old age, I expect. Cartographers usually enjoy long lives. It's such a peaceful and uneventful occupation.' They reached the street in which Schenck lived. He offered again to escort Estrella home.

'No,' she said. 'Go straight to your lodgings. I'm quite safe.'

'But the streets are dark – how can it be wise for you to continue alone?'

'Please, go. I shall finish reading your manuscript at home.' She bit her lip. 'If I finish it this evening, may I call to return it to you?'

Schenck thought of Frau Luppen.

'It may be a little difficult . . . But yes, of course.'

She wished him good night, and he left her. As he reached the door, he looked back to see Estrella still watching him. Then she turned and walked away, back in the direction from which they had come. Schenck's house was not even on the route to her home.

Inside, there was a smell of boiled cabbage. Frau Luppen came out of her apartment to greet him.

'Would you like something to eat?'

He declined, and went upstairs to his room. There he lit the lamp, and sat down by the window, at the table on which Pfitz had been created – his Pfitz; a creature possibly bearing no relation to the smudge which had erased Spontini. There was some meaning to all of this, but it was not yet apparent. Estrella had walked him home, then left him. Spontini meant something to her. They each had their secrets to keep. Would they ever be able to overcome these obstacles, and speak honestly to each other?

From downstairs, the odour of cabbage water was wafting up to him. He recalled the bristly pigflesh, and Frau Luppen's bosom close to his face. These images were enough to banish whatever appetite he may have had. He felt tired and vaguely nauseous. He fell asleep where he sat.

When he awoke, he guessed that an hour or two must have passed. The unpleasant smells downstairs had now found their home in the stomachs of Frau Luppen and Flussi. Schenck rubbed his eyes, and looked out of the window, into the darkness of the street. He saw a figure move.

He rubbed his eyes again, and looked more carefully. Someone had retreated into the shadows of a building. Someone was watching him. He opened the window, and considered calling out. Then the figure stepped forward. It was Estrella.

'What are you doing here?' his voice was a hoarse whisper, which still seemed to fill the silent street. She held out his manuscript for him to see. 'Wait!' he said, then went downstairs as quietly as he could to the front door. Estrella was waiting there when he opened it.

'I've brought it back for you,' she said.

A voice called out. 'Is that you, Herr Schenck?' Frau Luppen, behind the closed door of her apartment, sounded sleepy and uncertain. The Cartographer replied that he was only taking some air. He waved Estrella to go quietly upstairs, then followed her.

Now they were both in his room. When Estrella saw the sheets of blank paper on the table, he explained that

92

they were for a report. He offered to take her heavy coat, but she said she preferred to leave it on. She seemed distant and slightly awkward, as if her mind were somewhere else. She also declined his offer of a seat, but instead remained standing near the door which Schenck closed behind her.

'Here's the manuscript,' she said, holding out the bundle of papers again at arm's length. Schenck took them from her.

'Is something wrong?'

'No,' she replied. 'Forgive me. I'm a little tired, that's all.'

'You could have given me the documents tomorrow.'

'Yes. But I wanted to see you.'

Schenck felt as if she were pulling him towards herself with one hand and yet pushing him away with the other. Everything in her words and gestures seemed contradictory, driven by conflicting urges.

'You told me you were attacked the day before yesterday,' she said. 'Do you have any idea who your attacker may have been?'

'He came from behind, and ran off before I could see more than a dark figure escaping.' Schenck was unwilling to discuss the matter any further. 'Do you want more of Pfitz's story? I can bring it to you.'

'Yes,' she said vacantly. 'Yes, bring me more.'

'You said you liked the Author's style.'

'It has some interesting features.'

Schenck stood up and moved closer to her. 'Is it the kind of Author . . . whom you could love?'

She flinched. 'What kind of a question is that?'

Schenck went to the window. It seemed wise to change the subject. He opened his satchel and pulled out Spontini's book. 'Have you ever read this?' She took it from him, and her examination of it before putting it down again reminded Schenck of the look he had once seen on the face of a child, who came upon the corpse of a dog.

'I already told you that the author was unknown to me.'

'Are you sure that you know nothing about it?'

'Are you now accusing me of lying?'

'Forgive me. And please forgive me also for saying that I find your manner this evening strangely cold and hostile, as if I have wronged you in some way.'

'You will appreciate that a young woman who visits the lodgings of a young man is putting herself in a position which might, if she is not careful, prove to be compromising.'

Schenck moved still closer. 'Yes,' he said, 'I fully appreciate that. And I should like to know why you chose to come here, when you could just as easily have returned the manuscript to my office.' Now he was standing beside her, near enough to touch her arm, or kiss her. She lowered her head. He sensed that she was waiting for him to act.

Everything about this moment would remain clearly outlined in the memory of the Cartographer. The folds and contours of her dark coat, and the red flush of her cheek, like the map of a great and mysterious empire. The patient, thoughtful manner in which she stood with her head bowed, as if trying to hide her gaze from the shabby room, and her face from the man who stood next to her. When he remembered this moment years later, he would see two strangers. He reached out and held her hand. It was cold to the touch. She stiffened, but did not move away. He stroked his thumb against her fingers. Still she did not resist. He brought his face close to her cheek; surveyed that soft continent which smelled so sweet. As he kissed her, he tasted the fine down of her skin, and his imagination was transported into the limitless steppes of a foreign country. Now he held her in his arms; this thickly-clad figure, whose bulky clothes suggested frail delights deep within. Her waist was bending with the pressure of his arm around it, its shape defining itself beneath his touch, and her neck was bending also, and this new territory was yielding itself for exploration. His hands were finding greater courage, and beginning to roam over the rugged terrain of her coat, towards the warm expanse of her bosom.

Then, buried beneath her coat, his hand found something hard. 'What's that?' She tried to pull away from him, but already he had reached inside to retrieve the knife which lay concealed. 'What do you need to carry this for?'

She drew away, and pulled her coat tightly around her. 'The city is a dangerous place,' she said.

'It's very unusual for a woman to carry a weapon such as this.'

'It is also unusual for a woman to visit the lodgings of a young man. I felt it wise to be able to defend myself should the need arise.'

'And do you think it would have arisen?'

'It might have. Give me back the knife.' He handed it to her. 'Now good night. I hope that tomorrow you can bring me more of the manuscript about whose origin you choose to be so secretive.'

'Let me escort you home; it isn't safe for you to walk alone.'

'I think it would be even more unsafe for both of us if we were to remain together any longer. My knife will protect me from harm. I look forward to reading the next part of Pfitz. Perhaps when I bring it here tomorrow we shall both have learned to treat one another with greater decorum.'

She would not even let him show her out to the street, but crept downstairs alone, and left without a sound. Schenck felt that their uneasy meeting had been a terrible mistake.

But there was still Pfitz; the one link which held them together. The one reason why Estrella needed him. He sat down at the table, exhaustion creeping over him like a great heavy beast upon his back, and stared at the blank, hostile pages.

Chapter Twelve

COUNT: Wake up Pfitz!

PFITZ: (sleepily). What? Where are we?

COUNT: I don't know. I don't recognize this place.

PFITZ: I've never seen such a high ceiling in all my life. And pillars and statues everywhere. Could do with some more light though.

COUNT: Do you think we're dreaming Pfitz?

PFITZ: Almost certainly.

COUNT: Let's look round.

They are in a great marble hall. A flight of steps curves upwards before them. They ascend.

COUNT: I can make out glass cases over there. You know Pfitz, I think we've reached Rreinnstadt! We're in the famous Museum.

PFITZ: Too bad it's only a dream, sir.

COUNT: But tell me, is it you who is dreaming this, or is it I?

PFITZ: It's me sir, quite definitely. I always know when I'm dreaming, because I get a peculiar stiffness down one arm. It must be the side I sleep on.

COUNT: And yet I'm sure I'm really here. I can't be existing only in your imagination.

PFITZ: Perhaps we've both found ourselves in the dream of someone else. Who can say? But as long as we think we're here we might as well make the most of it.

COUNT: Let's try this door.

PFITZ: Alright. Handle's a bit stiff. I think it must be locked.

COUNT: There's a sign on it. Can you make it out?

PFITZ: (reading slowly). Salon of Irretrievable Experience. Best left alone, I'd say.

COUNT: Through here, then. I want to see the exhibits.

They wander amongst the glass cases; some of them empty, others crammed with objects. They reach another door. Its sign reads 'To the Library'.

COUNT: This is what we want, Pfitz. And it isn't locked. Follow me.
PFITZ: That corridor looks very dark, sir. I don't like the way it seems to descend into nowhere.
COUNT: Don't worry. Just stay close behind me.

The two walk together, down the long corridor which is lit only by feeble candles fixed alternately at intervals along the walls.

PFITZ: I do hope this is your dream sir; I'd hate to think that I was capable of imagining such a terrible place.
COUNT: Stop frightening yourself, Pfitz. We're nearly at the end – I can see another door ahead.

On opening this door, they find that they have reached the Library. Before them, brilliantly lit, an endless vista stretches of shelves crammed with books – shelves which extend so far upwards that it is impossible to judge their height, and which can only be scaled using the ropes and ladders attached to them.

PFITZ: Where are you going, sir?
COUNT: I want to conclude my search. It's only now that I can understand the real reason for our visit here – for our entire journey. I want to find Spontini.

The Count walks towards the shelves and quickly disappears amongst them.
 – Now we can find out whose dream this is.
 What do you mean?
 – If we follow the Count, then it must be his; if we stay with Pfitz then he's the one who is dreaming it all.
 But what if the dream is your own?
 – I couldn't possibly have a dream like this one.
 The Count rounds a corner, and someone grabs him from behind. He feels a knife at his throat.

COUNT: Please! You can't kill me. It's only a dream – you can't die in your dream!

ASSAILANT: You can if it's your last.

COUNT: Are you Spontini?

The Count is released, then turns to face his attacker.

ASSAILANT: I am not Spontini. But like you, I am searching for him.

COUNT: Explain yourself.

ASSAILANT: There were ten of us once. Then five, then two. And now only I am left. We were all looking for Spontini. We wrote his stories, his fantasies; we invented mythical places and peopled them with characters who might live in his imagination. We were all looking for him. What he was – whatever he was – was the common factor in all of our work. Somehow, out of that enormous diversity, he would emerge.

COUNT: But you never found him?

ASSAILANT: He always managed to elude us. We got close, on many occasions, but in the end he would evade us once again. The only thing we could say for certain was that he was very hard to track down – his work is so varied, so disorganized, that we often doubted whether he even existed at all.

COUNT: But you wrote these works yourselves – you and your colleagues.

ASSAILANT: We wrote, as a quill writes. The person who puts pen to page is no more than a channel for ideas whose origin and meaning he can never hope to discern.

COUNT: And what happened to all the others?

ASSAILANT: There was dissent, doubt, argument. Some of them didn't like the way things were going – the Aphorisms were hard work. A book should converge onto something; it should focus somewhere. But what was emerging was a book which diverged endlessly – a process without any prospect of resolution, or hope of completion. What we were discovering was not a single author, but a whole collection of voices without any common theme. It seemed that Spontini would die without completing his first work. These differences between us were only the beginning however. There were also personal conflicts. Our Chairman began to suspect that his wife was in love with one of his colleagues, though he said nothing. As our work continued, I could see that the tension we all felt was revealing itself in the writing we attributed to Spontini. Or rather, it was as if the spirit of Spontini was beginning to exert a malevolent influence over us. Our project was going badly. The Chairman called us all together for a meeting. 'This tale might have any one of several different endings,' he said. 'And its multiplicity is made all the richer by the fact that we still cannot be sure precisely who it is that the story concerns, in what time or place, and in what manner the resolution of the narrative should be presented. But I am aware – painfully aware – that our progress has at times been hindered by the vanity of some, the pride of others, by ambition and self-interest, and even by deceit. We are all the servants of literature. Without it, we are nothing. Let us not forget that no sacrifice is too great, if it will enable us to achieve our collective aims.'

Someone interrupted: 'What collective aims? We are all going in different directions; this book is all over the place. I suggest that we divide into sub-committees. We can't all keep working on Spontini.'

The Chairman waited until this outburst was finished. 'I agree,' he replied, 'that Spontini is a strange author, and there are many possibly contradictory aspects to his work. But we are all of us the sum of numerous contradictory parts. In this respect, Spontini lives within every one of us.'

Nevertheless, an argument ensued. In the end our team split. Some of us would continue to contribute material for Spontini while the rest would pursue new authors.

Some weeks later, I was walking along the street in

the evening when I came upon a terrible figure. It was the Chairman, his clothes in disarray, and blood on his hands. 'What have you done?' I asked him in horror, though I knew that the blood must belong to his own wife.

'This is where the story ends,' he said.

COUNT: How terrible. But what about your Reader; did you at least have some agreement on who your work was aimed at, in order that it might achieve some coherence?

ASSAILANT: Yes. Her name is Estrella. And she was the cause of everything which took place.

– No, he's lying!

Calm yourself, please.

– Let go of me. You must let me go!

A monstrous growling is heard, and a thundering like cannons being fired. Then a woman's voice is calling.

Chapter Thirteen

It was Frau Luppen knocking at his door. Schenck had not written a single line before sleep had overcome him.

'Are you alright Herr Schenck?' He opened the door to her. 'I woke up and noticed the light in the street, coming from your window. I thought you might have had some accident.'

This was a strange conclusion to make, but Frau Luppen's logic was unique, and consistent enough in its own way. She was dressed in her nightrobe, and held a lamp in one hand while Flussi was in her other arm. Schenck said that he was quite alright, but Frau Luppen was looking past him into the room, inspecting the bed, sniffing the air. She saw the table and entered. 'Have you been writing?' Now Frau Luppen was turning the blank sheets one by one.

'I intended to begin a report. I fell asleep over my work.'

'That's how fires start! What if you had knocked over your lamp?' She closed the shutters of the window. 'And it's so cold in here. If you don't burn yourself to death you'll probably freeze.'

Schenck had no idea of the time. His mouth felt crusty and dry, and he saw now that he had even drooled slightly on the uppermost sheet of paper. Frau Luppen looked tired, irritated and very ugly. Her hair was tied up with pieces of paper which made her resemble a huge child's toy, and her blotchy face was deeply lined. Only Flussi, it seemed, was able to maintain her appearance throughout the night. She panted on Frau Luppen's arm, her ribbon still in place on her head.

The landlady's annoyance was ebbing. Now there was a note of sympathy in her voice – of genuine concern. 'Why don't you go to bed and get some sleep? What is it that troubles you so much that you sit by your window all night?'

'I told you – the report.'

'Pah! Report indeed. I wasn't born yesterday, Herr Schenck; I know what it means when a man's behaviour becomes erratic, when he can't eat or sleep.' She lowered her voice, as if confessing a great secret, and she stared meaningfully at him with her bloodshot eyes. 'It's all because of a woman, isn't it?'

This strange round figure with an absurd dog on her arm had suddenly acquired great power; she was backed by the force of truth. What use was there in Schenck denying? Only the details remained unknown to Frau Luppen. He felt her gazing, with her puffy sleepless eyes, straight into his aching heart, and it was an unnerving sensation – almost as if he stood naked before her, and humiliated. Yet still he struggled.

'The report . . .'

She reached out her hand, and stroked her fingers across his cheek in a manner which was playful, teasing, and triumphant. 'Women are trouble, Herr Schenck.'

It was the first time he had ever heard her say something memorable.

Flussi yapped, as if in agreement. 'Come along then,' said her mistress (her mother, as Frau Luppen always called herself); 'Time for beddy-byes.' Again she looked at the Cartographer, a parody of feminine seductiveness. 'Sleep well.' Then she left him, and went back downstairs.

When Schenck lay down upon his bed, his slumber was too profound to admit any further dreams. Next morning he rose and went to work. Gruber had arrived before him; the two greeted each other curtly. Later, Schenck was busy with his maps when Gruber came and spoke to him quietly.

'What exactly is going on? These Authors and Biographers you're getting mixed up with, what's it all about?'

'I wish I knew, Gruber.'

'Well, if there's any money in it, just remember the help I gave you. And if it's anything illegal, then it'd be too bad for you if I felt inclined to tell anyone else about it.'

It sounded like a threat. Gruber's words aroused yet more new suspicions in Schenck's mind. Why should he have said such a thing? When Gruber left him, Schenck felt a wave of anxiety deep in his stomach. Unsettling memories returned, of his dream the previous night. He was lost, adrift – a tiny point on a great ocean lacking any co-ordinates by which he might guide himself.

Soon afterwards, it was Estrella who came to speak to him. She appeared at the door of the office, checked to make sure that no one had seen her or might disturb them, then came and stood by Schenck's desk. As he got up to greet her, he tried to decide whether it was joy or fear which he felt. Her expression was stern and business-like.

'I haven't been able yet to obtain any more of Pfitz for you,' he said.

'Who is this copyist of yours? Where is he?'

'You know I can't tell you that. If you'll only be patient.'

'He's a liar, a cheat and a fraud.' She threw Schenck's manuscript onto his desk. 'Pfitz is a myth, an illusion. What are you both trying to do to me?'

Schenck was confused. When he put out his arm to try and comfort Estrella, she angrily moved away from him before continuing:

'I prepared a biographical summary on Pfitz based on what you had given me so far, which went for processing. But word came back to me this morning that the Count definitely stays alone in Rreinnstadt. The testimony of the inn-keeper at the tavern where he lodges makes this clear.'

'But Pfitz is marked on the map. He sleeps on the floor beside the Count.'

'I think you should check your map again. If there is anyone called Pfitz then he isn't known to have anything to do with the Count.'

Schenck's face was lowered in shame. Estrella's voice sounded pleading. 'Why?' she said. 'What are you trying to do?'

The Cartographer summoned the courage to speak.

103

'The copyist is an acquaintance of mine. He invented the story of Pfitz so as to entertain you. So as to interest you. He loves you.'

Estrella was crying even before the Cartographer could finish speaking. 'Who is he? You must tell me.'

'I cannot. Not yet.'

'You must stop seeing him. Believe me, he could be very dangerous.'

'That's impossible. He wishes you no harm. He wants only to know whether you could ever find it in your heart to love him in return.'

If Schenck hoped to stifle the sobs which he found so unsettling, then this was not a wise statement to make. Fortunately, Estrella chose to ignore it.

'So much damage has already been done. I've got to hand in the rest of the details about the Count's journey. We've got to make sure that when they get to Rreinnstadt the two of them aren't seen together by the inn-keeper. If they are, then everything will become inconsistent and we'll be lost.'

Schenck was glad that she said 'we'.

'If you give me time,' he said, 'I can get more for you.'

'Tell your acquaintance that if he cares at all for me then he will have to make sure that when the Count reaches the tavern in Rreinnstadt Pfitz isn't seen with him.'

'How is he supposed to do that? Pfitz and the Count are inseparable.'

'Then Pfitz will have to die. He shouldn't have come into existence in the first place. You'll only be restoring things to their rightful order.'

Schenck was saddened by this, but felt he had no choice but to obey.

'I'll see what I can do.'

'We don't have much time. I'll come and see you again tonight. Give me whatever you can come up with by then. But if we wait any longer then I fear everything will be found out.'

She left.

So now as well as playing the role of author, Schenck had to don the mask of assassin also. It would be an onerous task. He began to think of all the many ways in which Pfitz might meet his death. Meanwhile, there was still another matter which needed to be investigated. He returned to the Literature Division, and went upstairs to the Authorship Office, which he now found open. A Clerk was dozing behind his desk. 'I'm looking for Spontini,' Schenck said. 'What can you tell me about him?'

The Clerk peered through the small silver-rimmed ellipses of his spectacle lenses. Then he began to consult his records, slowly and patiently, as if it didn't matter whether the task took him an hour, or a year. At last he gave a faint smile of success, and handed over the document he had found. It was a handwritten report, and it was clear at once that this had been Gruber's source. What Gruber had omitted was of no particular interest – trivial details and references. What struck Schenck immediately, however, was the handwriting. It was a familiar script in which the story was framed of Spontini's descent into madness – an even, elegant hand, gently sloping, which he recognized from a note he had received some days earlier. The handwriting was Estrella's.

Her denials were hollow – an attempt to deflect the Cartographer from the truth. She certainly knew all about Spontini. Why was she so determined that the Cartographer should not be able to discover her involvement? Again he remembered his dream, and wondered if it might prove prophetic; as if some truth had been revealed to his sleeping mind, which the waking one had previously chosen to ignore.

Schenck thanked the Clerk and left (his mind filled with conflicting theories, tangled speculations). As he went downstairs, he had only the vaguest awareness of the steps beneath his feet, or the great sweep of the stone banister. He returned to the Cartographical Office, and sat down again at his desk. His maps held no interest for him now. His mind was too troubled, his thoughts turbulent and confused. In the meantime, he must return to Pfitz's story. Could he really bring himself to murder his creation? He considered several ways in which he might bring Pfitz's life to an heroic end, yet each filled him with a pang of regret. There must be some other way to ensure that he would remain undetected by the scrutiny of the biographers and historians. Schenck began to write.

Chapter Fourteen

COUNT: Talk to me Pfitz, to pass the time while we ride. Why don't you tell me about your loves?

PFITZ: Ah sir, there's no point. I could tell you about Lotte, or Minne, or Constanza ... but when I think of all those stories, I only feel tired, and my head aches.

COUNT: I don't like to hear you like this, Pfitz. Are you unwell?

PFITZ: Perhaps I am sir. You know, I even had a feeling when I woke up this morning that an accident might occur at Rreinnstadt which will be my last.

COUNT: How can you say such a thing? You'll outlive me by many a year, I'm sure of it.

PFITZ: Even so, when I look back on all the women I've known, and all the fine things I've tasted, and all the places I've visited, I feel nothing except a strange emptiness, because I've lost them all.

COUNT: This melancholy is quite uncharacteristic. We'll consult a physician in Rreinnstadt.

PFITZ: Then my death will be a certainty.

COUNT: Don't say such a thing! Tell me a story; it'll take your mind off morbid thoughts. You still haven't finished your account of how you came to be born. Your father said he was at Brunnewald, didn't he?

PFITZ: And fought most valiantly there. But towards the end of the day he caught a bullet in the leg.

COUNT: A bullet which had, so to speak, his name on it?

PFITZ: Or else one which had someone else's name on it and was badly aimed. But do you really want to hear any more?

COUNT: Of course I do Pfitz.

PFITZ: Very well. After he was shot he was put in a cart and taken to the army doctor who said straightaway that the leg should come off immediately. When my father

107

heard this he wept and cried at the thought of losing the leg that was so dear to him, and he begged the surgeon to spare it. But the surgeon said that if he didn't amputate then my father would surely die of gangrene; he'd stake his reputation on it. My father said his leg was worth more than anyone's reputation, and he'd take his chances. The surgeon was surprised to hear such spirit from a young lad – for my father was still little more than a boy, remember – and decided to spare him the knife. For several days he was in a hellish fever, at the end of which the wound began to heal.

COUNT: As indeed it had to, in order that you might one day be born.

PFITZ: If it was ordained that my father should catch a bullet in the leg that day then it was also ordained that he should recover. And if it was an accident that he got shot then it was chance that he survived. Either way, it was just as well for me. Then once he was better he waited for the army doctor to see him again, who had wagered his reputation on my father dying, and he asked him what he made of it. My father thought the man would be shocked to see that he'd been proved wrong, but he only gave a shrug and said that medicine is not an exact science, and anyone can make a mistake. In fact it turned out he was a veterinary surgeon by training, and he said that had my father been a horse then the diagnosis would have been perfect. Anyway, he'd come across far stranger cases over the years – he'd amputated limbs that had grown back again, and seen babies born with two heads, and removed gallstones that had teeth and fur. And he'd encountered the diseases of the mind as well; like the soldier who thought he was a fish and got drowned in a rain butt, or the woman who couldn't stop singing. But the strangest case he said he ever came across was the man who fell in love with a shadow.

COUNT: Fell in love with a shadow? I should like to hear that story.

And so Pfitz continued. He was a young man – a student. Very poor, naturally – he had a dark little attic room where he would study at night by the light of a candle, and although there was a stove for heating he could seldom afford fuel.

He always took the same route to and from the university, down a succession of narrow cobbled streets; leaving in the early morning, returning at dusk. Looking up one evening he happened to notice the yellow light of a curtained window. And he saw a shadow moving on the curtain; a woman – the dark image cast by the lamp inside growing and shrinking as she walked about the room.

The next night he saw it again, and soon it became almost habitual for him to watch the shadow as he went by on his way home. He began to wonder who she might be, the woman hidden up there. Young, beautiful and lonely was how he imagined her. By day, the window would remain curtained, and he never saw anyone enter or leave the building. This only fed his curiosity. Soon it was no longer enough for him simply to glance at the shadow; he would pause to observe it, waiting in fascination for some clue as to its meaning. Before long he was spending hours at night in the street, looking up at the silhouette, which would disappear to one side, after a while come back, the form ballooning to fill most of the window with grey shade as the woman moved back towards the lamp, then becoming smaller, darker and clearer whenever she came near the curtain. The youth would wait, hidden in a doorway across the street, until at last the light would go out and he would return to his attic.

While performing this solitary vigil one night he finally resolved to take action. It was late, there was no-one about, and the light was still glowing high above him on the other side of the alley. He went over, looked furtively around him, then began to climb up the drainpipe of the house, his heart thumping in his chest. The window was above him, on his right – he could almost stretch his arm to the sill. He pushed himself a little higher – now the window was within reach. He gently pulled his sleeve down over his hand, raised his arm, and with all his strength plunged his fist through the glass. The noise filled the empty street. He grasped the curtain inside – his feet were slipping. He kept hold of the cloth – which alone was preventing him from falling – yet it was coming loose and he felt himself tumbling down, the curtain still in his hand. He crashed down to the street, fragments of glass all around him, and landed heavily on the cobbles. Without a moment's hesitation he got to his feet, put the curtain under his coat and ran home, never once looking back.

In the darkness of his attic, he had time to notice the pain in his leg, the blood on his hand. He brought out the precious cloth, let it fall open, and pinned it to the wall. Still it was glowing yellow, casting a soft light across the room, and there upon it was the shadow pacing back and forth, distraught. When he came near to try and soothe her, the shadow would vanish to one side, like a nervous bird in a cage, only coming back slowly once he moved away. He tried to touch it, to stroke the soft hair of the dark silhouette, or take hold of her arm, but each time the shadow retreated from his grasp. Eventually he lay back on his bed so as to observe from a distance the prize which his act of madness had won him, until in the early hours of the morning the yellow light suddenly went out – the curtain became dark again – and he fell into exhausted sleep.

When he rose he bound his wounds and went out, securely locking the door. At the scene of his crime, the window was now heavily boarded up, with no sign of life. That night he returned to his room to find the curtain again emitting its soft light. The shadow seemed a little calmer now, but still it would not let him approach.

So it went on for weeks. He brought her presents, said sweet things to his captive during her nocturnal appearances, but he knew he would never win her heart. Sometimes the shadow would shake a fist in anger, or weep silently. Mostly, she would simply look forlorn and listless. Perhaps sheer perseverance would wear out her resistance –

this was his only hope. Then one evening he came back with some flowers he had picked for her and was horrified by what he saw – on the curtain, a second shadow had appeared; that of a man holding his companion by the waist. Before his eyes, they kissed passionately.

The youth was dizzy with rage. He shouted, swore at the curtain; pleaded with his love, then cursed her, and the one who had stolen her from him. At last, in a frenzy, he tore the glowing curtain from the wall – the shadows still embracing upon it – ripped its glowing fabric and thrust it into the stove. It flared, and was gone.

He went out weeping into the night, crying for the love he had lost. He wept in the street and on the bridge over the river. He wept in the forest, beneath the stars, and as he looked down at the ground which was bright with the cold blue moonlight, he wept more bitterly still. For he saw that he cast no shadow.

COUNT: What am I supposed to make of that?

PFITZ: Make whatever you like sir. As my father used to say, the world is full of queer stories, and every one is true in its own way.

COUNT: He sounds like a strange character, your father.

PFITZ: If he had been anyone else then I could not have been his son.

COUNT: I suppose not.

At the end of the day Pfitz and the Count reach Rreinnstadt.

COUNT: That's the North Gate up ahead. Soon we'll be able to lay our heads down for a good night's sleep.

PFITZ: If we can find anywhere to stay, that is. Remember it's the Festival of the Swan, sir. Everywhere's bound to be full.

COUNT: A nobleman never wants for a place to sleep, Pfitz.

PFITZ: But his servant often does.

An hour went by during which they were turned away from several taverns which could not accommodate them.

Each time, Pfitz was sent in to enquire, and each time he came back out without having had any success. At the Red Fox, however, Pfitz had better luck. They had a room which had been booked, but which was now free since the guest had not appeared.

PFITZ: In that case, my master will take it. Is there also a cot in which his servant might sleep?

INN-KEEPER: The room is small, and fit for one person only. His lordship can't have any servants or guests with him.

PFITZ: Not even his valet? How is he to dress?

INN-KEEPER: It's a single room, and the Commission of Public Houses is very strict about these things. I wouldn't want to lose my licence.

PFITZ: Is there another room, where the servant could sleep?

INN-KEEPER: None whatsoever.

PFITZ: Or a shed, or a patch on the scullery floor? Or a cupboard?

INN-KEEPER: Not a chance. The Count can have a bed, but his servant will have to fend for himself elsewhere.

The Count was pleased that Pfitz had found him a place to stay, and seemed confident that Pfitz would somehow manage to sort out his own accommodation.

COUNT: There are hundreds more taverns in Rreinnstadt, Pfitz. Or there are some very pleasant bridges to sleep under.

PFITZ: Thank you for your consideration. I hope you will enjoy your stay. Though I should warn you that it's a rough-looking place – be sure to lock your door.

Pfitz described in great detail some of the stories he had heard of rich men being murdered in their sleep while on their travels, until eventually the Count decided that it might after all be safer for Pfitz to spend the night with him in his room. If Pfitz made his way in without being seen, he could sleep on the floor.

So now it is night, the Count is in his bed, and Pfitz sits cross-legged beside him, cutting his toenails.

COUNT: I do wish you'd stop that.

PFITZ: Shoe the horse tomorrow and the nails will cost you double. That's what my father always used to say.

– Can you tell us something more about this tavern in which they find themselves?

In proportion it is unexceptional; in facilities unreliable; in hospitality unacceptable.

– What unpleasant incident might have caused Pfitz and the Count to form this opinion?

The serving up, by a surly black-smocked ruffian, of a joint of beef fit only for a starving dog, upon an unwashed plate; so that the Count would have thrown it back in the man's face, if it had not occurred to him to smuggle it upstairs for his servant.

– Did Pfitz eat the beef?

Not only the beef, but the stale bread too.

– Did the Count go hungry?

Yes, with the words: Better to starve nobly than eat like swine.

COUNT: Make sure you don't flick any bits onto my bed.

PFITZ: I'm nearly finished, sir. The big ones are always the toughest. You know, I once heard about a man who saved them up – his toenail cuttings, I mean. Made model boats out of them. If you stick enough of them together, it's amazing what you can do. Strong stuff apparently, and easily worked. Not only that, though – he used to go round gathering up every bit of hair and fluff he could find, then he'd spin it and make clothes. And whenever he cleaned his ears . . .

COUNT: That's enough, Pfitz. Why don't you put out the light and lie down?

– What did Pfitz do upon hearing this request?

He gathered up the last cheesy moon-like crescents of shorn toenail between the thumb and index finger of his right (dominant) hand, went to the south-facing window and pushed it open, then sprinkled the fragments into the cold night air. After this, he extinguished the lamp and lay down in the darkness upon the room's hard floor, adjacent to and parallel with his master's bed, the distance between the two being one arm's length.

– What happened then?

They lay in silence for some time, until eventually the Count felt moved to speak.

COUNT: Pfitz, if anything were ever to happen to me . . .

PFITZ: Like what?

COUNT: I don't know. Anything. If I were to die, what would you do?

PFITZ: I'd find another master sir.

COUNT: You say it so calmly! How can you be so callous?

PFITZ: A man has to live, sir. You can rest assured though that I could never find a wiser, gentler master than you.

COUNT: Thank-you Pfitz. Did you have many masters before me?

PFITZ: Several, but all quite unmemorable. Except for the Baron, who had a very pretty wife.

COUNT: Were you in love with her?

PFITZ: I'll say! You know, I've often observed that love grows in inverse proportion to the attainability of its object.

COUNT: That's very profound.

PFITZ: It was my father who pointed it out to me.

COUNT: Did he love your mother?

PFITZ: Only until he married her. Then he spent the rest of his life pining for a girl he met in a farmhouse the night before Brunnewald.

COUNT: I think you've told me that story already. Good night Pfitz.

PFITZ: Good night sir.

Chapter Fifteen

Schenck was interrupted by a knock on the door of his office. He expected to see Estrella again, but it was a man who entered after Schenck called out in reply; an unknown man who made the Cartographer give a start. He should have been busy with his maps, instead of writing, and he felt like a naughty child whose wrong-doing had been discovered.

The visitor wore a long black coat. He was not unusually tall, but powerfully built, while his broad hands could belong to a stone-mason or a wrestler – the slightly flattened appearance of his features lending further support to the latter possibility. Yet his face seemed intelligent, and his thick unruly hair gave him the air of a philosopher.

'I have been watching you,' he said. Schenck was alarmed by this. Had he come from the Superintendent's department to chastise the Cartographer for neglecting his work? 'I must warn you that you are in grave danger.' He took the seat which he was offered, and then continued.

'You have shown an interest in the Aphorisms of Vincenzo Spontini. I was leader of the team which produced that book. My name is Konrad Weissblatt.'

He did not allow Schenck the opportunity of expressing his pleasure at meeting him, but instead continued.

'It was two years ago. A very unhappy time. Not at first, you understand; we were all very pleased with Spontini. He was going to turn into a fine author. But everything went wrong. And all because of a woman named Estrella.'

Schenck trembled as he listened.

'She was compiling Spontini's biography. We sent her what he wrote, she sent us details about him; it was the usual constant exchange of information. Our work created his life, and was at the same time created by what we knew of his life. It's a process which always works, as long as none of the participants allows his or her own personality to interfere. But that's what happened. None of us had met the biographers; we simply delivered our work for them to examine, and for Estrella to compile her notes. She read Spontini with great interest. With too much interest. And she fell in love with him.'

Waves of jealousy rose in Schenck's throat as he heard Weissblatt say this. He continued.

'Her love grew into an obsession. And she transferred it to the unknown writers who had created Spontini. She made the mistake of identifying us with our fictional offspring. One day I was working in my office when she appeared at my door and introduced herself. Then, though she didn't even know me, she declared her love. Spontini had given voice to thoughts and feelings which had lain unexpressed within her; he was a man of sensitivity who understood the deepest workings of a woman's heart; he was a passionate genius who had changed her life. As far as she was concerned, despite all my protests, she was speaking to Spontini himself when she addressed me.

'Then she embraced me, and begged me to take her as my own. I pushed her away as gently as I could. I wanted to make her understand the madness of what she was saying, and yet I did not want to hurt her. I thanked her for her kind words, but said that I (by which I also meant Spontini) was already married, and could not return her love. Her face reddened, and she rushed out.

'I thought that might be the end of it. But next day, when a batch of documents arrived for me from Biography, I found amongst them a letter from her. It read: *If Spontini's wife is the only obstacle, then she must die.* You can see that she was quite unhinged. I felt that my only safe course of action was to try and ignore her, rather than risk encouraging her madness. But soon afterwards I received the news that Spontini had murdered his wife. It seemed that the deranged Estrella was carrying out her plot to win him – or should I say to win me? Fact and fantasy had become blurred and intermingled in her mind.'

'Did you report her actions to her superiors?'

'I had no wish to add to the misfortunes of this pathetic creature. Nor did I mention anything to my colleagues or even to my own wife. That is now my greatest regret.

'I received further messages begging me to love her, all of which I ignored. We continued to work on Spontini, though we were all now filled with sorrow at the news that the course which had been charted for Spontini's life would end in murder and insanity. None of the other writers could understand how this might have come about, and I did not dare tell them that it was all because of a woman whom I had spurned. Now Spontini's own work was becoming darker, tinged with anguish, jealousy and madness. But the terrible plot in which I had become ensnared was still not over.

'I remember the day all too clearly. I was working at home, and needed to refer to another writer's contribution to the *Aphorisms*. I did not have a copy of the piece, and so I decided to go to the Library of the Literature Division in order to consult it. My wife offered to accompany me, so that she could take the air. As we drew near the Library, I realized that we were being followed.'

'Estrella?'

'Of course. I didn't want my wife to encounter her. We went inside, and I knew that at some point I would be confronted. So I told my wife to go on ahead and locate Spontini's unfinished work, telling her where she might find it. I had other business to attend to, I said.

'I waited in the corridor, expecting my enemy to appear at any moment. But some time went past without there being any sign of her. My wife also was taking rather a long time to find the book for which I had sent her. It occurred to me that Estrella could have entered by another door and challenged her. In a panic I ran into the Library, calling out my wife's name. I hurried to find the place where Spontini's book would be shelved.

'My wife lay slumped on the floor, stabbed to death. I cried out for help, as if my cries might revive the woman I loved more than life itself. I cried out in the hope that Estrella would return and kill me too. But she had fled.'

'Was she arrested?'

'Let me explain to you the cunning resolution of her plot. I was found at my wife's side, holding her hand and mumbling incoherently, such was my shock. I told them about Estrella; they challenged her, and she denied all knowledge of me. None of my friends or colleagues knew of any connection between the two of us; but they did know that my behaviour recently had been erratic, as if I was troubled by something. And they knew that Spontini's work had become disturbed and violent, even though the other writers had tried to maintain his calm, so that in the end the Biography Section had deemed it necessary to make him go mad. And Spontini's own work had suggested to them the idea that he would kill his wife out of jealousy. It was, you see, a perfect plan. They had no choice but to find me guilty of murdering my own wife.

'My plea of insanity was accepted. I was sent to an asylum, where it quickly became apparent to my carers that I was perfectly healthy. After two years the scandal had died down sufficiently, and it was deemed safe to allow me my freedom. Now I could begin to try and put right some of the evil deeds which had been perpetrated. I can never bring back my wife, but I can at least try and prove Estrella's guilt, clear my name, and clear the name also of Spontini.'

'What do you mean?'

'The murder of his wife was fabricated by Estrella. She framed him in the same way that she framed me. And now I believe she may want to use you to cover up her crimes. You see, in her biography of Spontini, the murder is committed in a Rreinnstadt tavern, the Red Fox . . .'

'That's where Count Zelneck stays!'

'Yes, and Estrella made the murder take place in the Count's room. He is the only witness. Now that she is writing his life, she need only make sure that the Count does indeed see the crime being committed, and then her lies will pass into the accepted facts of history.'

'But Spontini's name is erased from the map which shows the room. Why is Pfitz there?'

'I don't know of any such person.'

'I tried to find information on him for Estrella, but had to resort to making it up myself. I'm writing more for her now.'

'Perhaps it's all part of her plan. But it could also provide us with a way to thwart her . . .'

'She wants me to kill Pfitz.'

'I don't understand how she intends to complete her scheme, but you must ensure that Pfitz's presence – whoever he is – prevents the murder of Spontini's wife. She visits the Count's room during the night.'

'Why?'

'Because she is afraid of her husband – groundless fears which were stirred up by Biography. Nevertheless, she takes refuge in the Count's room.'

'While Pfitz is there too?'

'You'll just have to fit them all in somehow. Spontini arrives and challenges the Count to fight; the rest is up to you.'

Schenck was stunned and bewildered by what he had heard. Estrella was using him as an instrument in a sordid scheme of revenge which had already led to a woman's death and a man being incarcerated for two years. Other incidents recalled themselves to him – the attack in the street, Gruber's 'accident', the hidden knife. He felt a shiver of fear, a sad longing, a nostalgia for the innocence in which he had believed. There was a part of him which loved Estrella, no matter how much she might hurt him. And yet he would have to be strong. He spoke:

'I'll help you in any way I can. Estrella will visit me tonight; what do you want me to do?'

'Listen carefully. First, you've got to make sure in your writing that the Count never witnesses any murder. That will at least prevent Estrella's falsehoods from disseminating further. Try to discover her plans, but do not mention me or allow her to suspect that you know anything. Should she attack you, you must be prepared to defend yourself. She is a strong woman, and you shall have to fight for your life. I must leave you now. Be brave. Good luck.'

Weissblatt's words left Schenck numb. If he tried to denounce Estrella, would she make sure that he was incarcerated, just as the poor writer had been?

The *Aphorisms* were beginning to make sense to him now. A team of writers trying to produce a coherent novel, but their leader filled with anguish and remorse. Spontini's madness, a terrifying inevitability brought about by the actions of a deranged woman. He would continue with the story of Pfitz later, but now he opened the *Aphorisms* once more, at a later page than the one he had left earlier, deep within its spiralling story, and he began to read.

Chapter Sixteen

The river is in torrent, because of the rains which have fallen upon the city, and on the hills far upstream for days without end. The rain still falls, more lightly now – a mere drizzle, but enough to soak anyone who remains outdoors for too long. In these last days the river has become brown and swollen – yellow where the water is shallowest; like the colour of parchment, or old skin. As I watch it rush below me, I see the static ridges and folds which form as it passes beneath the arches, like hair intricately tressed and knotted; an unchanging pattern of flowing water.

I am not the author of these words. I, Vincenzo Spontini, am a colony of writers; a city of ideas. My work (which shall forever remain unwritten) is an amalgam of the various tastes, styles and interests of those whose ideas would seek to flow into the space which my literary identity is to occupy. The Spontini who drinks a glass of wine, who walks along an avenue lined with rustling poplars, who savours the beauty of a sunset; these are all different men, each one distinct, each one existing only for a moment, or co-existing within a single fragile location.

I have observed that the world is made manifest through a multiplicity of forms. And one might characterize this multiplicity by saying that any person is in fact an infinity of individuals, that any point in space is an infinity of points, that any story is an infinity of stories.

There exists a view that words correspond with the world in the way that a glove might fit a hand. For every thing, there is the word which names it; for every thing, there are words which enfold and define it, which describe and illuminate it. Words which are appropriate, and those which are not. This is not my own view however. Words form their own world; their links with that other world of the senses and of our own experience is at best a tenuous and uncertain one; the bond between word and object is as flimsy as a spider's silk, and like beads of morning dew, these threads bear the burden of association, of unshared convention, of ambiguity. Words do not coagulate around objects so as to enclose and contain them, but suggest a perspective which is infinite and treacherous.

This analogy of the spider's web has its limitations (like all analogical reasoning), but also its attractions. We could see language as a trap which we spin in the hope of catching something which must forever elude us. And we must remain perpetually vigilant, unless we are to become ensnared in our own creation.

But again, implicit in such an idea is the belief that there is something out there to be caught. Can we be sure that it is not the case that in the absence of language all things become meaningless, in the way that objects are colourless when not illuminated?

Everything is water. Not only the river; the bridge on which I stand is another kind of water — and the statues which line it, they too are a further form of the same substance, the same eternal principle. The grey clouds which drift and hang over the city are an obvious manifestation; but also the air I breathe, and the time which has passed while these thoughts have flowed through me, and even those thoughts themselves; everything is water, floating in water, sustained by it.

In that other time (the time of which some of us still long to write, but with a passion which is inflamed now only by nostalgia), there was a sense (an illusion) that those words which emanated from us came from a single point, a centre — radiating outwards as if projected through a lens. And these words, in the mind of those who read, might once more converge to an image of that original point. We were then, in those days, nothing more than an optical instrument — united and co-operating in our efforts — through which the reality of the world could be refracted and focussed.

This co-operation, it now seems, was little more than a temporary illusion; a convenience, held together by vanity, greed and the desire for fame. Hollow things, all of them, yet who can deny ever having chased one of those fugitive spirits? So that now instead of focussing the world, we can do nothing except magnify the differences which exist between us, the conflicts and disagreements.

I believe that I am remembering something, but this may be another trick which they are playing on me. I believe that I am about to act under my own volition, but I cannot be sure whose hand moves the pen, or my eyes and mind as I read. I know only that I am made manifest through many diverse voices which bear little relation each to the other. What I am is a collection – an anthology – of incomplete, disconnected ideas. Is any man more than this?

The mind cannot be understood as a single entity. It is more like a community; an assembly of intercommunicating parts. Where then, you might ask, does the 'self' reside? Is it simply one of those parts, undistinguished and no better than any of its fellows?

Like me, the statues are being eaten by moisture. Their stone faces are creased and streaked by dark rivulets, the unending imperceptible process of erosion and decay. One day they will be worn smooth; their faces, their limbs transformed back into inhuman rock. Then the bridge will be lined by two rows of featureless boulders. Like the statues, and the city itself, I am being worn away by the rain, eroded by it, until all that will be left is a stone whose inscription becomes day by day less intelligible.

While I was thinking of these words, I had a vague awareness of other thoughts (the hardness of the stone bench beneath me; the imagined comfort of my study; other images which they try to send me). Is it possible to have a thought without being aware of it? Is it possible to have many selves, each of which fails to recognize the others?

I imagine the following situation: A group of writers is working together to invent the works of a certain author. Since this author does not actually exist, there can be no true centre from which their work emanates – instead, what they have is a diffuse collection of ideas amongst which they must seek some kind of coherence. What is the factor which is common to all of the fragments they produce? This is the problem which must be solved; since that common factor (supposing it to be capable of being found) is the character of the author which those writers are trying to create. It is not a story which they are writing, but rather the author of a story. Or is this simply another idea sent by them to trick me?

In the folds and tresses of the water beneath me, I imagine other inscriptions; intangible, yet somehow more enduring. This is the bridge on which so many people have stood, yet the river I see now has been witnessed by no-one else before me. I am the first to see this water gathered here — these accumulated raindrops — and I shall also be the last. Might the bridge itself be a kind of river? Is the bridge on which I stand really the same one on which others have strolled, arm in arm on a summer's evening, or on a crisp morning in spring? Like the river, the bridge is in a perpetual state of transformation; of decay and destruction, of replacement and renewal. I am the first person to stand on this bridge, and I shall be the last.

One of them shows me what he has written. Together, we try to decide how this piece will be fitted into the final work — we try to decide what place it will occupy, and what it might tell us. He watches me in silent anticipation, as I read his words.

The writer who invents a story invents also the teller of that story. And the one who tells a story invents his listener. They have invented Spontini, and Spontini has invented me. And now I must try to reinvent all of them once more.

And just as the bridge is in reality a particular process of change and exchange, so the stone figures must also recreate their identities with each passing moment. A gradual diffusion, an evaporation of their form, their limbs, their faces, until nothing remains, and what gave them life has been spread uniformly over the entire city. A grain of sand is brushed by a raindrop from the eyelid of St Anthony; it falls onto the flagstones, is washed into a

puddle and remains there until the sun returns, the puddle dries.
The grain is blown by the winds over the city, and out into the
fields where it falls on brown earth. One day it will be caught up
in an ear of wheat, it will find its way into a loaf of bread, into
the stomach of someone who will then have eaten a part of the
statue which stood, for the briefest of moments, on a bridge which
itself was no more than a flickering vision, a transient thought.

In my cell, I read these words which they have given
me. I try to imagine where I shall place them, in the
finished text. I try to discover whose story it is in which I
have found myself; whether I am a central character, or
else little more than an incidental episode in the life of
someone else. But the voices still disturb me, they distract
me, and make it impossible for me to think (or might it be
the case that the voices are my thoughts?) If I can only
conquer them, if I can only find the right way to do it, and
the right moment. Then there will be silence, and they will
disturb me no more.

Chapter Seventeen

Schenck could understand now the process of fragmentation by which Spontini had been destroyed. He imagined him, deranged, imprisoned, doubting his own existence; and he thought of his creator Weissblatt, tortured by the obsessive attention of Estrella.

The book seemed to take as one of its themes an idea which the Attendant had expressed to Schenck during their last conversation; that a personality, an identity – a mind even – can somehow emerge from parts whose co-operation is almost accidental. And not only thoughts or feelings, but meaning itself, the very fabric of the world, might be things whose apparent complexity is a kind of mirage. If Schenck could find some satisfactory answer to all his questions, must that answer necessarily have been put there by someone, like a message in an envelope, waiting for him to read it? Was the solution he sought already written up above, or was his investigation somehow creating the very object of its enquiry? To doubt, to suspect; this can make the innocent seem guilty, it can turn the most harmless and trivial event into a crucial piece of evidence.

Schenck tried to work on his maps. A map is a clarification of the world, a rationalization of its hopeless confusion, in which everything is disentangled, codified, classified in inks of various colours. A map is the fulfilment of an impossible dream; to render the world on paper. Schenck looked at the General Plan of the City of Rreinnstadt; the beautifully engraved representation of a concept, a place which existed nowhere. Impossible perfection.

He remembered what he had been taught by one of his supervisors when he had first been apprenticed to the Cartography Division. The Supervisor showed him a map of a certain Mediterranean island, and asked Schenck to find out the length of its coastline. Schenck used a piece of thread, as he had been taught, to follow the curving line of the island's boundary, and then after he had measured this he calculated the actual distance. The Supervisor told Schenck that he was nowhere near the correct answer. He then showed him another, larger map, far more detailed than the previous one, and asked Schenck to try again. The task was much more difficult now. Where before there would have been a straight segment of line (along certain bays, for example), there now proved to be jagged inlets, coves, irregularities which made him twist the thread further, so as to follow precisely the boundary which he was trying to measure. So that when he now calculated the length of the coastline, his answer was much greater than before. Suppose, the Supervisor said, he were to go to the island, to try and measure the actual distance exactly. He would have to follow not only every inlet and headland, he would also have to meander around every rock, boulder, the smallest pebble even. His measurement would be an endless process of digression, as his ever-increasing accuracy took him towards a final answer infinite in magnitude. The Supervisor's conclusion? That the world is a treacherous web of imperfections and anomalies; that a close study of it will surely lead one into divergent conclusions, into paradox and chaos. Only in Rreinnstadt, in the pure abstraction of that unreal city, could perfection be conceived.

The more Schenck learned about Estrella, the more it seemed that to comprehend her would be a task which would forever elude him. In his mind she was growing beyond all bounds, mystery within mystery. To possess her body now would be the poorest reward, a mere triviality. To understand, to explain – this was what he sought. He wanted her to be like one of his maps, her soul laid out and charted before him, its every motive located and defined.

His thoughts were abruptly disturbed. Gruber had come, ostensibly to ask about watercourses. This, it soon became apparent, was little more than an excuse. Eventually Gruber's intentions manifested themselves.

'Who was that man who came to speak to you? What did he want?'

Schenck tried to invent a reason for Weissblatt's presence; a routine errand, the clarification of an obscure problem. Gruber's reaction showed that the poor attempt only confirmed his suspicions, but Gruber seemed prepared to accept Schenck's explanation.

'And how are you getting on with Spontini?'

Gruber's question had an air of self-satisfaction; as if his only purpose in asking it was to display what he already knew. Schenck still regarded Gruber as a threat, a rival — even though he now had to force himself to abandon his pursuit of Estrella. He did not want to be drawn by Gruber's remarks, and yet his colleague was pursuing the subject.

'You said he was on one of your maps,' Gruber continued. 'Which map would that have been?'

To try and evade this interrogation would only arouse Gruber's interest still further.

'He visited Rreinnstadt once,' Schenck told him, 'or at least I think he did. The name was erased. He came to believe that he didn't exist, that he was a character written by someone else.'

'Which is perfectly true, of course.'

'Yes. So that really he was far more sane than most people.'

Gruber made to leave. 'Perhaps you're working in the wrong Department, Schenck.' He went out.

At the end of the day, Schenck walked back to his lodgings. When Frau Luppen asked him if he wished to dine with her, he replied in the affirmative, without even listening to the sound of his own voice. Soon he was sitting opposite her, with a bowl of stew before him. The foul-smelling meat was plumbed with tubes of gristle interwoven amongst the tough black strands of cooked flesh. Schenck thought of the plump arm of the woman he watched, as she bent over the work of eating; he thought of her thigh, and the great triple sack of her belly and breasts. To be nothing, to believe oneself to be nothing. What would this feel like? Could it be that he himself was no more than an illusion in someone else's mind; that the love he had imagined himself to feel for Estrella was a poor joke, told for others' amusement? He felt as wretched and dead as the overcooked meat in his mouth.

'Aren't you hungry? It's the old malady again, is it not?' Frau Luppen had stood up to collect his abandoned bowl. She was leaning low over the table – as close to its edge as her girth would allow, and stretching to lift Schenck's bowl, her bosom hanging like two enormous droplets of congealed tallow. She was taking far too long to pick up the bowl. She rested her hands on the table and looked up at him, her face not far from his. She looked into his eyes, challenging his gaze to leave hers, to direct itself at her body. Schenck could feel her breath on his cheek.

If he did not exist, then it did not matter what he did. If his life were no more than an imperfect dream – flawed and inadequate compared to the life of Rreinnstadt and its inhabitants – then his actions were dictated not by volition, but by the motion of some other urge, beyond himself; some natural force for which right and wrong would have no meaning.

And yet he did not move. And Frau Luppen straightened herself, and took the bowls away. Schenck watched her retreating mass. She was no longer ugly to him; he watched with a cold fascination, as he tried to reach some decision, some logical conclusion. An infinite coastline was unravelling itself in his mind; a thread which he was trying to follow.

Frau Luppen had come back. She said nothing, and went to wind the clock. Schenck got to his feet. She was standing with her back to him, her fat fingers struggling with the delicate key. Schenck assessed the outline of her rump, the thick folds of her skirt. He thrust his hand deep into the pleats.

Frau Luppen's response as she spun round, the key still in her fist, was not so much a slap as a punch – the sort which sailors sometimes land upon each other in dockyard taverns – and it sent Schenck crashing to the floor. The key had cut his face – not badly, but just enough to bring to an end all his philosophical speculations, all his cold abstractions. Yes, he did indeed exist. And what he had just done was not only reprehensible, but might cost him the roof over his head. He got up and left, too ashamed even to apologise. He went straight upstairs.

In his room, he could hear Flussi's barking far below, a kind of laughter. He felt angry and humiliated. And he wondered what he would have wished to do if it had been Estrella winding the clock, and not Frau Luppen. Estrella would visit him later. He had the next part of Pfitz ready for her, but there was still more to do. He felt a wave of contempt, of loathing for his futile task and the woman for whom he had begun it with such high hopes. But then he remembered Weissblatt, and the noble duty to which he had pledged himself. He sat down at his table, and began to write once more.

Chapter Eighteen

In the middle of the night, Pfitz is woken by a noise outside. At first he takes it to be the crying of a cat, but as he listens he realizes that what he hears is the sound of a woman in tears.

He rises quietly from the floor on which he has been sleeping, being careful not to disturb the Count, and looks out of the window. In the shadows below, he can make out a female figure. He opens the window to see better, and she steps forward into the moonlight.

PFITZ: (in a whisper). What's wrong?
WOMAN: Help me sir, for I don't know what's to become of me.

– Who is this woman?
Someone no doubt who will bring misfortune to Pfitz and the Count.
– Why do you say that?
Because, as Pfitz's father used to say, 'women are trouble.'
– That's a most foolish and unkind thing to say. Would you say that I have ever caused you any trouble?
A great deal. You have made me tell you the Author's story of Pfitz, and all you have done is keep interrupting and criticising, so that I fear we may never reach the end.
– Then I shall remain silent, while Pfitz lets that poor lady in out of the cold.
He goes down to the front door, careful not to make a sound which might waken the inn-keeper, and allows the woman to come inside. Then he takes her up to the Count's room, where Pfitz finds his master sitting up in bed.

COUNT: What's going on? Who the blazes is she?

PFITZ: Quiet sir, she needs a place to stay. She says she's in danger.

WOMAN: Forgive me sir, but if my husband finds me I'm done for.

Pfitz lights the lamp, and when the Count sees how pretty their visitor is he feels slightly less annoyed.

COUNT: Do sit down, madam. I'm sorry there isn't a comfortable chair, but the edge of my bed should make a good enough seat. Who is this husband of yours that you're so afraid of?

WOMAN: He is an author by profession, sir. And believe me, no worse fate can befall a woman than to be married to a writer. Every minute of the day is devoted to his vocation – if he isn't putting pen to paper then his work is in his head, so that I am left all but ignored. He has had countless affairs with women he's invented, whom he loves far more than he could ever care for me, since I'm nothing more than a distraction or an irritation when he wants to get on with his scribbling. You wouldn't believe the cruelty I have to put up with, in the name of his art.

PFITZ: He sounds like a very selfish fellow.

WOMAN: They're all the same.

COUNT: And to think that he could be so neglectful of one as beautiful as you! These pretty hands, or your cheek as white as porcelain, and how soft!

WOMAN: You flatter me, sir.

COUNT: Does he not know that he's the luckiest man on earth, to be able to put his arm around that lovely waist . . .

PFITZ: (aside). I never knew the old boy had it in him . . .

COUNT: Or kiss those sweet lips . . .

PFITZ: Calm down, sir. Let's hear what she has to say.

WOMAN: I think all my husband's stories have finally gone to his head. He's been acting very strangely. In fact, I believe he may be trying to do away with me.

COUNT: Whatever gives you that idea?

WOMAN: I have to make fair copies of his work, since his handwriting is so bad. That way I get to read everything he produces. And I don't like the way this new book is turning out; all about someone who kills his wife – the cheek of it! Look, I've got part of the manuscript here with me; you can read for yourselves.

Pfitz and the Count examine the text which she shows them.

PFITZ: I think you're right, madam. Your husband's off his head, and he wants to kill you.

COUNT: That's enough, Pfitz. If this young woman really is in danger then it's our duty to protect her.

PFITZ: Sounds risky sir. Never come between a husband and wife. I learned that from Charlotte a long time ago. If she stays here and her husband finds her then he'll kill all three of us, and my premonition of misfortune will have been completely fulfilled.

COUNT: How very satisfying for you.

PFITZ: So I suppose I'd better make sure I finish telling you how it was that I came to be born. It was all because of the Corn Tax . . .

COUNT: We don't want to hear this now!

WOMAN: But I should very much like to. Do please continue.

PFITZ: Thank you madam. My father was a glazier, you know. He could just as easily have found himself apprenticed to any other profession, but after his heroic exploits at Brunnewald he met up with someone who offered to teach him the trade, and so my birth was brought one step nearer. It was towards the end of his three years of apprenticeship that they introduced the Corn Tax. It was a very unpopular law – taxes always are – and there were meetings and clubs forming everywhere to protest about it. One evening a friend invited my father to go with him to one such meeting, and out of politeness he accepted.

The meeting was held in the basement of a fishmonger's shop. My father and his companion went down a narrow staircase to the cold room where the session was already underway. They took their places at the back, and my father found himself sitting next to a pretty woman.

The speaker was a fiery young rebel with long hair who waved his arms around a great deal and talked about everything under the sun apart from the Corn Tax itself, and soon everyone there was clapping and cheering – even my father, although he only joined in because he was watching the woman beside him and thought it wise to copy every response she made.

But then the meeting was interrupted. There was banging and shouting upstairs – the militia had arrived to see what was going on. An officer was saying something about riotous assembly and the protection of the populace, but in fact everything had been perfectly well behaved until they appeared and started clattering downstairs, a whole platoon of them, telling everyone the meeting was over and they would have to leave. The fiery rebel said they had every right to continue, and when the militia men took hold of him he put up a struggle. Others joined in, and soon it was an all-out fight. Even my father's friend joined in.

My father, on the other hand, had no taste for violence. He'd already witnessed more than he could stomach at Brunnewald. He grabbed the girl who had been sitting beside him and said they had better get out. So they began to make their way back up towards the street, along with others who were trying to escape. And then in the room below they heard a shot being fired.

One of the militia men had let his gun off, wounding a young man. Now it was a wave of panic which swept my father and the girl up those stairs and into the street, trampling over anyone who was unlucky enough to stumble. And the street itself was also full of people now; no-one knew quite what was going on, but stones were being hurled and more shots were fired. A barricade was already being put up.

'In here,' the girl said, and she pulled my father through an open doorway, into an empty shop. It was dark in there, and they could hear all the shouting and commotion going on outside. My father decided it would be best to hide, and found a pile of sacks beneath the counter, on which they could both lie down together.

COUNT: A smart move.

PFITZ: They passed the time most pleasantly, I don't doubt. Later my father woke up and found himself alone. He looked for the girl, but couldn't find her anywhere.

WOMAN: Was she your mother?

PFITZ: Of course not. He never saw her again. I said my birth was due to the Corn Tax, but you could also say that it was due to my father being such a heavy sleeper, because if he had woken earlier then he might have persuaded the girl not to leave him, and so my father might have married her instead of my mother, and his excellency the Count would have had to find another servant since I would never have appeared in the world.

COUNT: So you must feel very grateful to those comfortable sacks and your father's sleeping habits.

PFITZ: Indeed I do, although my father may have felt differently about the matter.

COUNT: But how then did the Corn Tax riot bring about your birth, as well as the annihilation of all those rival children which your father could have had?

PFITZ: It was a big riot, and a lot of windows got broken.

COUNT: Good business for your father, then.

PFITZ: Next day he was sent to do some repairs in the street. My father jumped out of his cart into a puddle, and splashed a woman who was passing. If he had not been a glazier, and if there had been no riot, then he would not have been there. And if there had been no

135

puddle for him to land in, there would have been no argument between him and the woman, and if there had been no argument she would have walked on and they would never have come to know each other and fall in love and marry, and then I would never have been born.

COUNT: Don't you think that it might have been fate which arranged for your father to survive a terrible battle, to become a glazier, survive an equally terrible riot, jump into a puddle, and thereby to encounter your future mother?

PFITZ: That was my mother's view. She sometimes used to say 'Isn't it wonderful that fate should have enabled me to meet the man who is exactly what I was looking for?' to which my father would say two things: first, that it would only be remarkable if my mother had had no choice in the matter of whom she married, and second that if she had never met him then she would now be with some other man, telling him how wonderful it was that fate should have led her to the best of all possible husbands. My father, on the other hand, was left to dream of all those other lives he could have led, with all the girls he had lost.

WOMAN: That's right, a typical man; always dreaming of what he hasn't got instead of being grateful for what he has. My husband's just the same.

COUNT: I hope we don't get the opportunity to meet him and find out for ourselves.

PFITZ: We're in for a long night sir, so we'd best make ourselves comfortable.

COUNT: Perhaps the young lady needs to lie down?

WOMAN: The floor will suffice for me. You might like to pass the time by perusing my husband's manuscript, while your servant diverts me from my troubles with his stories.

So the three of them settle down, and wait to see what the night will bring.

136

Chapter Nineteen

Schenck heard a sound in the street below his window, and looking out, he saw Estrella. He hastily picked up the sheets he had written and hid them in his satchel, the ink scarcely dry, then went downstairs to let her in. There was no sign of Frau Luppen, and he was able to take his guest quietly up to his room.

Schenck's impression of Estrella was greatly altered. He now saw a woman deranged; a dangerous monster who had gone so far as to kill Weissblatt's wife. But could it really be so? Now that she stood before him once more she looked fragile and harmless.

'I have some more for you.' The Cartographer brought out the papers he had just finished writing. Estrella eyed them suspiciously.

'Is Pfitz dead yet?'

'No. Does it have to be this way?'

'There's no choice. Whoever your author is, he must find a way to get rid of Pfitz.'

'You treat a man's life so casually.'

Estrella laughed, then remembered the need to maintain quiet. 'This is only a work of fiction, have you forgotten?'

'If it were not, would you show any more respect?'

Estrella looked puzzled and annoyed. 'What is that supposed to mean?'

Schenck wanted to challenge her, but remembered Weissblatt's advice. He did not pursue the matter. 'Just because Pfitz isn't seen in the tavern, it doesn't mean that he doesn't exist. Pfitz hides and avoids being spotted. He's marked on a map . . .'

'I told you, there is no Pfitz.'

'And what about Spontini's wife?'

Estrella looked startled. 'What do you know of her?'

Schenck could not hold back any longer. 'It's time you

told me everything you know about Spontini. There must be a good deal to tell, since you wrote his biography.'

'No,' said Estrella, 'it's you who must explain yourself. The one who has been giving you Pfitz's story – what is his name?'

Schenck refused to discuss the issue, which only made Estrella persist all the more forcefully. 'You must tell me. It's Weissblatt, isn't it? He's using you to strike at me.'

'I know of no such man.'

'Then who else can it be who has written all of this?'

Schenck thought silently for a moment before speaking. 'The author is not Weissblatt. I shall reveal to you his true identity, if you will first tell me who this man is whom you fear so much.'

'Very well. You're right, of course, about my connection with Spontini. I worked on his biography. And when I saw you in possession of the book that is so hateful to me I felt sure that Weissblatt must be involved.

'It all began two years ago. He was the leader of the group of writers who were producing Spontini. He delivered some documents to Biography, and when he met me . . . he fell in love with me.' She looked down, as if in shame. 'He regarded me as the reader for whom all his work was intended; the *Aphorisms* were his excuse to see me, and became a way of expressing his desire. Now I believe he's doing it all over again, with Pfitz.'

'No, Estrella, that isn't so. Weissblatt has got nothing to do with Pfitz. I wrote all of it myself.'

Estrella looked at him in amazement. 'You? How could you?'

'Because I wanted to be able to see you. Rather like Weissblatt, I suppose. Because I thought I was in love with you.'

When she looked at him, her eyes seemed filled with sadness. 'And are you still?'

Schenck drew away from her. 'I don't know. But what happened to Weissblatt? Did you return his love?'

'No, never. He . . . his mind was unhinged. I believe he was sent to an institution where he could be taken care of.'

Schenck sensed some evasiveness in Estrella's responses. He still doubted her, still needed to put her explanations to the test. 'Did he have no-one who could care for him? Family perhaps? A wife?'

'None that I know of.'

Still she was looking down at her hands, still she was hiding some terrible secret.

'In what way did Weissblatt become unhinged? Did he become violent or dangerous? Did he kill anyone, perhaps?'

Estrella gave a start. 'No. What would give you such an idea? No, he was a pathetic man, but not violent. They locked him up for his own good. Are you sure you've never seen him, and that he has nothing to do with Pfitz?' There was pleading in her voice; she had raised her hands to her face. Schenck took hold of them.

'I told you, I wrote it all myself. For you.' Her hands were in his now, and her face. He felt the softness of her hair where it fell across her cheek.

She said: 'What did it feel like, when you thought you loved me?'

There was a knock on the door.

'Are you alright in there, Herr Schenck?' It was Frau Luppen. 'I thought I could hear you talking to yourself. You aren't about to have another turn are you? Why don't you let me in?'

By his outrageous behaviour towards Frau Luppen a little earlier, Schenck had already ensured his own eviction. Even so, he did not want Estrella to be seen. He glanced around the room for a place where he could hide her, but there was little scope. He motioned her to get under the bed.

'Will you open the door, Herr Schenck?'

Estrella stared at him in startled disbelief, but another knock on the door and Flussi's yapping made her respond to the Cartographer's command. She got down on her knees and crawled out of sight. Schenck opened the door.

Frau Luppen entered and looked around the room, then

139

at Schenck. Now that she was facing him she seemed lost for words, trying to decide how to frame her speech. She moved to the centre of the room, looked back towards the door, and waited until Schenck closed it. She stroked Flussi while she gathered her thoughts.

'What happened earlier . . .' she said.

'It was an act of folly.' To have it discussed within Estrella's hearing made it all the more painful.

'But my response too was most . . . unworthy of me. I was so taken aback. I realize that your recent injury may have affected your judgement – that such lapses may occur. That it may be necessary to be lenient, and to excuse them. Even to tolerate them.' She had moved closer to him. He could smell fresh perfume. 'Were you hurt when you fell?'

'No, not at all.'

'But I cut you.' She was reaching out towards his face. He drew back.

'A scratch, nothing more.'

As she approached, he retreated. It was like a dance of scorpions. And it was progressing in the direction of Schenck's bed.

'Can you forgive me, Herr Schenck?'

'It is I who must ask forgiveness.'

'Oh but you have it, please believe me.' She had taken his hand now into her own plump grasp. There was nowhere left to retreat to; Schenck was toppling, she followed still. They both landed very heavily; Frau Luppen upon Schenck, who gasped both in surprise and because he was winded by what had fallen on him; and Schenck upon the bed which groaned and sagged with the unprecedented load. As for Estrella, her silence beneath this scene of turmoil made Schenck wonder if she had been killed instantly by the force.

Warm kisses were landing upon his face. Flussi was licking his hand. It was a moment of confusion, and not without its delights. 'You did not need to be so afraid,' she was saying, 'or so abrupt.' Their bodies were rocking from one side to the other, so that whether or not Estrella had

140

survived the first shock, she now was in danger of being ground to dust.

'Frau Luppen no, we mustn't.' It was the thought of Estrella which made him say this, though he also felt now a malicious pleasure, and the possibility of revenge on the biographer who had resisted him so consistently. But it was a sound outside, at the front door, which made them stop. A visitor was calling.

Frau Luppen got up and hastily rearranged her clothing. She was out of breath, Flussi was yapping, but she managed to compose herself sufficiently to go and see who had arrived. In fact it was Gruber. Schenck heard his colleague's voice downstairs, inquiring after him, and so he too went down; leaving Estrella – if she was not already flattened – to crawl out from her hiding place and wait for him.

Schenck received Gruber in Frau Luppen's apartment. The landlady – still flustered and in some disarray – went to 'sew a button', and left them alone.

Gruber began by asking for some more information on drainage systems, but this was no more than a pretext.

'This fellow Spontini that you're so interested in – what's all that about?' Gruber had been to the Literature Division to do some research of his own. He had borrowed another copy of the *Aphorisms*, which he brought from his bag. 'Do you know the people who wrote this?' Schenck said that he didn't. 'Their boss was locked up for murder.'

Schenck could scarcely conceal the shock of this blow. Had Estrella lied after all, then? Once more her innocence was shattered before his eyes, once more he saw a dangerous criminal. Schenck still did not mention his conversation with Weissblatt, but he needed to know everything which Gruber had discovered.

'There were no details; only that the leader of the writing team killed someone and got put away for it. But you still haven't told me why you're so interested in Spontini.'

'That doesn't matter,' said Schenck, pulling the book from Gruber's hands. And as he began to leaf through it, reading the disjointed text, it soon became clear that this version of the *Aphorisms* was not the same as the one upstairs in his room, where Estrella still waited.

Chapter Twenty

I watch the river rush below me, and I see the static ridges and folds which form as it passes beneath the arches; an unchanging pattern, like hair intricately tressed and knotted. Like her hair. The bridge: this is the place where I shall find her.

I no longer know which of us is writing these words. That other one, the other Spontini, is the one who will remain. He is the one who ought to write, and about whom one ought to have written. I, on the other hand, am no more than his instrument. Each day I sit at my desk and watch the movement of the quill. I like the smell of the ink, the texture of fine paper. He cares for none of these things – or if he cares for anything, then it is with the disinterest and disdain of one whose every movement, whose every action is made not for personal pleasure but for posterity; for greatness and the heritage of our literature. I have tried on many occasions to escape him, and yet I can see that always it has been he who is the fugitive, and my only claim to significance (or even existence) is in my pursuit of him.

He will die young, yet live forever. I shall grow old, and then be obliterated and forgotten. He will be discussed, commented upon, argued about. Scholars will ruminate his wisdom, artists seek to represent the curve of his features in a space which he never occupied, since the only place in which he existed was the imagination of those whose faith and toil gave him life.

Long ago, I tried to heal the wounds which injured us all so deeply, the quarrels and disagreements – I tried to repair the damage, to soothe the pain. I failed. And I can see that whatever lives in him, and wherever he continues his life, comes precisely from that pain; that without the bitterness, the tears and even bloodshed, there would never have been anything. The one thing which emerged from us, the single thing which identified us, and hence our work, was our mutual enmity. And so the man we invented is a creature of discord; alienated from himself, and whose every whim or urge is a reaction to some other whim or urge, elsewhere in his soul. A man whose only purpose in creation is so as to have the subsequent satisfaction of destruction. Or rather, so as to be able to exercise with characteristic disdain his right to destroy.

I loathe him, and yet without him I am nothing.

And if I were to climb now onto the parapet of this bridge, this fleeting cloud of moisture, to climb as I have often thought of climbing, and look down through the swirling drizzle at the waters which churn beneath me, and if I were to prepare myself to fall, then would I find in that moment between life and death something more permanent, more durable than the cascade of images, one melting into the next, which this city and my existence within it have become?

In my cell, I have had the opportunity to try and organise my thoughts on paper, though this does little to make them any more convincing to me. I am still haunted by the conviction that everything is in some sense false, and every attempt to understand or theorize about the world and our condition in it is doomed from the outset to ultimate contradiction. Even so, there are certain statements which I feel tempted to propose, albeit tentatively. I am beginning to suspect that meaning is not a property which can be reached through a process of reduction. It is something emergent; something which arises in a manner incapable of being reduced to a sum of parts.

I say that a sentence 'means' something to me. Must it then be the case that each word of it means something smaller, and their sum constitutes the meaning of the sentence?

I see a familiar face. Would each part of that face be equally familiar? Would the eyes alone, or the mole beneath the ear, or a single strand of red hair convey a corresponding fraction of the meaning I derive from her face in its entirety?

Another image, like a grain of sand blown into my eye: her figure, seen through a billowing veil of mist, standing at the furthest end of the bridge. About to cross, to walk out onto it, past my own forgotten form, which must seem to her as lifeless as all the other statues which she hardly notices. She too is nothing but water, nothing but a particular kind of river, whose trickling course, whose eddies and idle corners must remain forever a mystery to me, forbidden and beyond reach.

Consider the following situation. You are sitting now at your desk. You like the smell of the ink, and the paper, and the leather chair which you find so comfortable. You like the texture of the paper, and the squeak of the nib as your pen moves across it. They have sent you another piece which purports to be by him, and hence to identify him. Already you feel you know who he is, what he is, and yet every new addition to him makes him less familiar; makes him less like the figure you wish to create for yourself. And yet he continues to grow, beyond anything you may have hoped for him. His personality is a thing you thought could be controlled; modelled in an image of your choice – this was a vain hope, and he will break free from the bonds with which you had wished to restrain and confine him. His words make him, and he makes you. Soon, he may grow to find you dispensable.

At the nearer end of the bridge, I see that other man – that other statue. Our three rivers met briefly, their waters mingled for an instant, for the briefest of moments, before running their separate ways. I see his face as it appeared when I killed him.

I am not the author of these words – I too have looked for him (for them). I see them within me, in the darkness when I lie down upon my bed of straw and close my eyes. I see them creating me, and creating all those others whom I may yet become.

I console myself with a quotation which may have been written by one of them: 'I know that everything in the world deceives me constantly, by its subtlety, its complexity beyond understanding, and by its being in reality part of a uniform whole which is incapable of reduction and comprehension. I know also that the mind which operates within this body constantly deceives itself, in the sense that it creates for itself images which, if not wholly false, are nevertheless hopeful distortions of a world which was never meant to be inhabited by it. I know that the world knows me, and I know nothing.'

And the motion of the river beneath me is another impossibility. At any given instant the water does not move, and so at every instant it is standing still. I see the static patterns; the folds and ridges through which the water appears to flow, and I think of Leopold as I might have left him, lying on his back in the snow, a bright line of blood tracing the contour of his chin. At every moment in time we are no different from a lifeless corpse. Our life is another kind of impossible motion. Another kind of water.

I shall leave others to argue over definitions and interpretations. For the time being, I look forward to the moment when the other *you* encounters the other *me*, as you round a corner in darkness, slightly afraid perhaps of what the night may conceal, and you feel my arm around you, suddenly from behind, and the knife held at your throat – at your throat, and yet at mine also, since we are in reality a single person; we are different parts of the same impossible person, who now sits in his cell and contemplates a death which will be as infinitely multiplied as the self-similar reflections of two parallel mirrors. Spontini will die, and I shall live forever. I shall die, and Spontini will live forever.

I climb onto the parapet of the bridge, and I remind myself once again of the paradox. A bullet flies through the air – in a second, it will travel from the barrel of my pistol to my victim's chest. In half a second, it will only fly halfway. And during an instant of time it flies no distance; but hovers, stationary, between leaving and arriving. Between life and death. Then if, at every instant, the bullet travels no distance, then surely the bullet cannot move. There can be no motion, no body lying on the snow, a bright trail of blood running over cold white skin; no body falling, like a stone, from the parapet of a bridge; no stars and planets above us, moving in orbits which fix our paths forever. There can only be water; stationary, eternal, and flowing in an endless river whose cold substance is ridged and folded, and tressed like the hair of a woman, and whose coldness as I dream now of entering it — coldness beyond sensation — is itself another kind of flowing and mixing, of sinking and submerging, of living and dying.

My crimes are the crimes of those who make me. What they have been trying to tell me — the messages they have sent me — may have been an attempt to warn me. I know only that they have been escaping from me constantly, while I have tried in vain to discover them, and to understand their intentions. They live within me; their words make me and yet I try to flee them.

Is this a memory or a premonition? I see again the blade, and soft unfaithful flesh, and blood on my hands. I run through dark streets, still pursued by those who would seek to write me, to correct me, to unwrite and erase a half-formed thought, to rephrase an urge which was most sincere in its first drafting. I feel myself being cornered by the language which defines me, and the literature for which I was created. I try to tell them that it is enough, and I can stand no more. I believe (perhaps this is another of their tricks) that I see one of them; in the darkness I come up against his startled form and perhaps he will realize now that his own life also has been no more than a fleeting vision, a figure glimpsed in the ill-defined region between one image and the next in an endlessly descending multiplicity of reflections, identical yet diminishing, one within another. And I say to him, as I have always said and as I shall say again and again, like an echo multiplied indefinitely between parallel walls:

This is where the story ends.
This is where the story ends.

Chapter Twenty-One

'I don't understand,' said Schenck, 'how there can be two different versions of the book. It's as if it's still being written, even after it exists on paper. And the writers – you say the leader was imprisoned. Who did he kill?'

Gruber did not know, but the possibility that Estrella had lied to Schenck continued to gnaw at his heart. He could no longer see his colleague as a rival; he wanted only to discover the truth.

'Gruber, we must get to the bottom of this. Estrella, the biographer, is upstairs now in my room.'

'What, the redhead? You old devil!'

'Quiet, we mustn't let Frau Luppen hear. If what I fear is true, then Estrella may be very dangerous. Come with me, and we shall confront her.'

This sounded to Gruber like a very interesting prospect. But when they reached Schenck's room, Estrella was gone. Schenck looked under the bed, and even in the tiny cupboard (much to Gruber's amusement), however it seemed that Estrella had slipped out while they had been talking.

'We must find her!' Schenck took his overcoat and led his colleague back downstairs to the front door.

'Shouldn't we say goodbye to your landlady?'

'No, this is none of her business. Try not to make a sound as we leave.'

It was cold and dark outside, and there was no clue as to which direction Estrella may have taken. Schenck remembered when she had stood at the end of the street as he walked to his door; it was that end of the lane which he decided to approach. Then they rounded the corner, and began on a route which was haphazard, although their pace was brisk.

'I met the one who wrote Spontini. He's called Weissblatt – he visited me in my office yesterday.'

Gruber cried out: 'My God, so that's who he was!' Now he felt able to make another disclosure. 'He visited me also. It was about a week ago – he showed up at the Cartography Division and wanted to look at some maps. I asked for a letter of authorisation but he had none. I shouldn't tell you this Schenck, but he offered me a purse of gold crowns.'

'What did he want to see?'

'I don't know. I went elsewhere and let him get on with it – if he was caught I didn't want to be involved. When I saw him come to visit you I got suspicious – it seemed as if you were both involved in some kind of plot.'

'We are, Gruber, but it's a plot which I don't understand at all. Estrella murdered Weissblatt's wife and he was imprisoned for it. Now he wants to clear his own name, and Spontini's as well. Or else he's mad and obsessed with Estrella. But then why did she tell me that he didn't kill anyone?'

Gruber could hardly keep pace either with Schenck's walking, or with his summary of the case. But it was made more for Schenck's own sake; an attempt to go through an argument and find some logic in it, some meaning.

'We'll never find her, Schenck. Don't you think it might be best to give up and go home? Whatever is going on between those two, why not leave them to it? If you ask me, Estrella is nothing but bad luck. Look what happened to me when I walked her home.'

'No, let's separate. That way there's more chance of finding her.'

'And what should I do if I find her?'

'Don't let her get away. Call out so that I will know where you are.'

Then Schenck sent Gruber away, and watched him disappear into the darkness. There was still no hint of where Estrella may have escaped to. He continued on his random path, and after half an hour he was weary but still determined to continue. He came to the river, and on the bridge he saw a lone figure. At last he had found her.

She was standing as if waiting for someone. The moon

149

was beginning to break through the low clouds, and by its light the Cartographer could watch Estrella as she shifted now and again, turning or walking a few paces, to resist the cold. She had not seen him. Then, while she looked towards the other end of the bridge, Schenck crept closer, walking onto its broad path, and hiding behind a statue whenever Estrella seemed about to look round. In this way, he was eventually able to come within striking distance.

The moon still shone brightly. Schenck waited until a large cloud began to cover it, the fringes of the cloud glowing white, then fading as the moon's face disappeared. Now it was dark enough. Schenck leapt out from his hiding place, and took hold of Estrella from behind, grasping her left arm tight in his hand, while her right flailed and struggled. She was trying to turn round to see her attacker, she was reaching for something. She brought out her knife, and swiftly cut Schenck's hand. He pulled back and saw a line of blood, dark blue against his skin in the faint light. Now Estrella could see who she had wounded.

'Schenck!' She lowered the weapon. 'Are you badly hurt?' He was wrapping his handkerchief around the cut. She offered her own as well. 'You shouldn't have surprised me like that. I might have killed you.'

'What are you doing here?'

'Can you not tell? I'm waiting for Weissblatt.'

'He arranged to meet you?'

'No. But he will come. And then perhaps we can bring this whole terrible episode to a close, one way or another.'

'You told me he didn't kill anyone. Why did you lie to me?'

'If I held back the truth it was only for your sake. The one who died was named Leopold. He was a member of the team which produced Spontini's book. I met him while writing Spontini's biography.' Estrella turned and looked out over the parapet of the bridge, at the water churning beneath. 'We fell in love.'

Schenck could not resist the agony of hearing more. He urged her to continue.

150

'Weissblatt became obsessed with me, as I told you. He had begun to identify himself with Spontini so much that he saw me as his own wife, and Leopold as his unfaithful servant.'

'So he killed him?'

Estrella gazed down at the white crests of water just visible in the darkness. 'They fought a duel with pistols. Leopold was no marksman.'

Schenck remembered what he had read. 'It's like the book.'

'What do you mean?'

'Leopold, and the duel. Spontini mentions them in the *Aphorisms*.'

'I think you're mistaken. Weissblatt's confusion of his own identity with that of Spontini didn't go quite so far as that.'

But when Schenck explained what he had just read in the copy which Gruber showed him, the solution became clear. 'He must have rewritten the *Aphorisms*,' said Schenck. 'Weissblatt is trying to rewrite Spontini's life, and his own. He must have been my attacker in the street, when he tried to take the book from me. And the map – he erased Spontini's name so as to try and hide the murder. It all makes sense to me now. But why do you think he'll come here?'

'This is the place where Leopold died.'

Schenck reached out to her with his wounded hand, but still she was gazing at the dark water.

'Weissblatt knows he will find me here. When I learned that he was free again I swore that I would never rest until I faced him, so that I could bring this terrible story to its end. But I also realized the danger he posed. First your colleague was attacked by him.'

'Perhaps because he knew about Weissblatt's involvement with the map.'

'And then you started bringing me all these stories of Pfitz, and I felt sure you must be one of his agents.'

'Is that why you left me waiting for you for so long?'

151

'Forgive me, I was afraid. And yet it was hard for me to believe you could be my enemy. And if you were innocent, then I had to protect you from danger. I even stood watch beneath your window, in case Weissblatt should attack.'

She was looking at him now with eyes full of trust. All his doubts had gone, his fears had flown away. He kissed her, and it was an embrace filled with hope and forgiveness. They were disturbed by a sound at the end of the bridge.

'He's here!' Estrella pushed Schenck away from her, and stood waiting with the dagger held behind her back. Weissblatt was coming towards them, a menacing figure in the moonlight. He drew near, and spoke to Schenck.

'What lies is she telling you?'

Schenck said: 'No, Weissblatt. You are the liar. You don't even know who or what you are.'

'My name is Spontini, and you are the wretch who has tried to steal my wife.' Now Weissblatt leapt towards Schenck, and the two became locked in a struggle. Estrella could only look on, unable to intervene in case she wounded Schenck.

'You aren't Spontini!' Even as they fought, the Cartographer tried to reason with his opponent. 'He doesn't exist; he's a fiction.' Weissblatt fell back against the parapet of the bridge. Schenck loosened his grip, and the two men stood facing each other.

'I know everything,' said Schenck. 'I know that you've been altering maps and books in an attempt to change Spontini's life. But you can never succeed; the facts are written, and cannot be undone.'

'You're wrong. I already have succeeded – or almost. One man alone stands in my way – the one who claimed to see Spontini kill his wife. I mean Count Zelneck. I shall kill you, and I shall kill him. And then I, Spontini, will be free.'

'How do you mean to kill the Count?'

Estrella interrupted: 'He's right; Spontini does kill the Count in Rreinnstadt. I've known that since I began his biography.'

'You mean the purpose of his journey is to be killed?'

'Yes,' said Estrella, 'but not before he denounces his murderer.'

Schenck still did not fully understand. He asked Weissblatt: 'What about Pfitz – the name you wrote on the map, after you erased Spontini?'

'There is no Pfitz,' said Weissblatt. 'My alteration of the map was hasty – I had to act quickly before anyone might come to disturb me. The mark I removed was the body of Spontini's wife, lying on the floor beside the Count. It was her name which I erased. But there was still a smudge left on the map. I pencilled an explanation beside it. *Pfütze*. A puddle. You misread my writing.'

So now at last Schenck knew the truth behind Pfitz. He was no more than a poorly labelled puddle. And he had accompanied his master on a journey which would end in death.

'You're sick, Weissblatt. You need to go back to the hospital where you can be looked after.'

Weissblatt launched himself once more at Schenck. It was a final, futile gesture by a man who could no longer believe even in his own existence. The two men fell against the low parapet; Weissblatt trying to push Schenck over. It seemed as if his powerful frame might be too much for the Cartographer. But then Estrella gave her assistance – she was grabbing at Weissblatt's legs, making him lose his balance, so that now it was he who was toppling, reaching out in desperation. His body slumped heavily against the parapet, and then over its edge.

Weissblatt was able to grab hold of the stone ledge as he fell across it, leaving him dangling from the bridge, his strong hands clasping at the stone. Schenck called desperately: 'Give me your hand.' But Weissblatt was staring at him with a look of calm resignation.

'This is where the story ends,' he said. Then he loosened his grasp and fell into the rushing waters of the river, where he was lost from sight.

Schenck and Estrella held each other closely. They

walked back across the bridge, and through the streets, neither able to speak. The horror of what they had seen lay in its inevitability, as if Weissblatt's entire existence – the life in which he no longer believed – had been no more than a preparation for its final gesture.

They went back towards Schenck's lodgings, and as they approached they heard laughter inside. Frau Luppen was in her apartment, talking gaily, while Flussi yapped excitedly. Looking in discreetly at the window, Schenck saw Gruber nestling in her enormous lap like a baby, Frau Luppen stroking his hair as she spoke. The two of them would, no doubt, be very happy together.

Schenck and Estrella went softly upstairs to his room. Both were quiet, subdued, and shocked by the terrible event they had witnessed on the bridge. And Schenck was also troubled by what Estrella had told him earlier. To ask her about it now, after all that they had seen, seemed almost callous. And yet he had to know more.

'Tell me about Leopold,' he said. 'What was he like?'

Estrella stood by the window, looking out into blackness. 'He was . . .' She did not continue. Was she afraid of hurting Schenck's feelings? Had she forgotten what he was like? 'He was like a child.'

Schenck stood up, took her arm, and watched a tear form and roll onto her cheek. 'What do you mean?'

When she spoke, it was as if to herself; as if Schenck were no longer there. 'He looked younger than he really was. And his hair was so soft. His voice was gentle, and even, and when he told one of his stories he could take you into another world.'

Schenck could feel her arm in his, and he could feel himself losing her; he could feel her heart drifting away, floating out into the impenetrable depths of space where Leopold's soul now dwelt – just as Leopold himself might have written (or was it Weissblatt?), when he told the story of the Prince and his Astrologer. Schenck could never win Estrella, he saw this now. He had invented the woman with whom he fell in love. That other Estrella, the

154

one born of a fleeting moment in the Biography Division, was no more than an illusion, lovingly nurtured. Here now was the reality. But if there were two Estrellas, might there not also be two Schencks? One who stood and watched the flight of his dreams into darkest oblivion, while another could know at last the joy he had hoped for?

She turned towards him, and the tears they felt on their cheeks as their faces met belonged equally to each of them, or to neither. They moved silently to the bed and lay down upon it, and when at last Schenck saw Estrella's body, naked and white beneath him, he saw a continent mapped in infinite detail, although it would remain forever unconquered. It was an imaginary landscape, a conceptual country; soft pastures on which to speculate, rich forests in which his mind could wander endlessly – unreal forests, unreal cities, like jewels; the firmness of a nipple resisting the flick of his tongue, a mountain peak which would vanish forever as soon as his imagination might begin to falter. Everything was held trembling beneath him purely by the will to believe. Rreinnstadt, Estrella, the world, or Schenck himself – these were all nothing more than beautiful dreams, sustained by hope, and the fear of oblivion.

At last they slept, and later when Schenck woke briefly he saw on Estrella's face still more tears, as if she were crying for Leopold even in her sleep. And then he wept too; for Leopold, for Estrella, for Weissblatt. He wept warm tears, and they made him feel light, and free. To live in your dreams – who can wholeheartedly condemn the man whose only happiness lies in such retreat? Was Weissblatt really mad, or had he in fact shown the true way? Schenck had lost Estrella – the Schenck who made maps, who walked to his work each day and ate his lunch from the table of an atlas placed upon his lap. That Schenck would grow old, would fade away, and would take with him the sweet memory of this night. But there was another Schenck, one who might live in Rreinnstadt, who might reach higher. One who might truly attain life.

The Cartographer did not exist, he now could see it, except as an instrument to create that other story. He had already begun it; all that was needed now was its final chapter. Estrella would wake later, and read his words, then take the manuscript to be incorporated into the eternal life of Rreinnstadt. And then Schenck would dissolve; his remaining mortal life would be of no further consequence. All that would matter would be the day far in the future when his own name, and Estrella's, would be carved together on that great cenotaph in Rreinnstadt, commemorating its creators. The day on which their souls would become linked for all eternity.

Schenck rose from his bed, quietly so as not to disturb those who still slept. He could hear Estrella's soft breathing, and the whistling snores far below of Frau Luppen, who lay locked in the arms of the stifled Gruber. The whole world slept. And Schenck sat down by the light of a candle, to write the last chapter of Pfitz.

156

Chapter Twenty-Two

Once more I hear the babble of many tongues, the appearance of communication. Language is a most subtle illusion, a deceptive form of behaviour. We do not seek meaning in the running of a horse, or in the sniffing of a dog. But a man speaks, and we seek some answer, some resolution, as if his speech should be an activity wholly different from that of any other animal, such as running, or sniffing.

COUNT: I can't make head nor tail of this.

It is late at night. Pfitz and Spontini's wife sit nearby, as the Count reads the manuscript of her husband's book.

COUNT: I prefer something with a good plot, where things happen. And there are characters you can relate to, and scenes you can understand and visualize.

– Me too!
Oh no, here we go again. Will you please let the story of Pfitz and the Count reach its conclusion?

COUNT: I can't work out who this story is supposed to be about, or what happens, or why.
WIFE: Then let me explain it to you. It's about a group of people who get together to write a book, but then they all fall in love with the same woman and start to argue amongst themselves, and they decide to settle the matter with a duel. One's called Weissblatt, and there's another called Leopold, and they meet on a snowy winter's morning to fight for the heart of the woman. It's so romantic, it almost makes me cry just thinking about it!
COUNT: I don't know if I've reached that part yet.
WIFE: They take the pistols from their seconds, then stand back to back. You can see the steam coming from their mouths as they breathe, and their white faces in the cold.

157

Then they begin pacing in the snow; it crunches beneath their boots as they walk. One . . .two . . .three . . . They turn and take aim. The guns go off. Crows fly in a great flock from bare trees. There's a nice line about their rising forms against the white sky. Leopold lies dying, with a thin line of bright red blood running from his mouth. Weissblatt walks away.

COUNT: I don't remember reading anything about Weissblatt or Leopold.

WIFE: Maybe you haven't been following it very carefully. It was my own husband who wrote it, and I copied it all out for him, so I should know. But now he wants to change it all. In the first version Weissblatt is arrested and charged with murder. My husband wants to rewrite it so that Weissblatt escapes.

COUNT: And why does your husband want to harm you?

WIFE: He's found someone else. I know it from what he writes. He tries to hide his feelings from me, but his own stories give him away. Now I'm just an obstacle in his path. If he finds me he'll kill me, I'm sure of it.

COUNT: Not while I'm here he won't. The man's utterly mad – anyone can see it from his book.

There is a noise outside.

PFITZ: What was that? (He goes to the window and looks out.) There's a mean looking fellow down there.

WOMAN: My God, it's him!

COUNT: Pfitz, go out and talk to him. Make sure he doesn't come in and find us.

PFITZ: Master, of all the commands you have ever given me in the many years we have been together, that is surely the most painful for me to carry out.

COUNT: Are you then going to disobey me?

PFITZ: Since my every action is commanded by you, and your every action is commanded from above, there's little point trying to argue. Out I go. Wish me luck.

The Count and Spontini's wife watch from the window.

158

After a while they see Pfitz appear in the street. He approaches Spontini, and they talk. It seems an amicable conversation, during which Pfitz takes great pains to point this way and that, as if giving his listener directions to some distant place. In the tavern, the two onlookers strain to hear what is being said.

WOMAN: I think he's saying something about how he came to be born.

But then things take a turn for the worse. Spontini becomes agitated. He looks up towards the window.

WOMAN: He's seen us!

With one great blow of his arm Spontini lashes out at Pfitz, knocking him to the ground. Then he approaches the door of the inn.

WOMAN: We're done for.
COUNT: I hope he doesn't waken up the whole place. What a scene!

Soon their own door is pushed open and Spontini stands before them; a tall man, powerfully built, and with a sword on his belt.

SPONTINI: What's going on in here? What are you doing with my wife?
COUNT: Please, I can explain.
SPONTINI: Address your explanations to the end of my blade. (He draws his sword.) Foul misprints! Heinous errata! I shall erase you both from this page!

He stabs his wife first, who falls dead on the floor. Then he turns on the Count.

SPONTINI: You too must be edited from my story.
COUNT: Is this, then, the sad reason for my journey here?
SPONTINI: Draw your sword, if you wish to die like a man.
COUNT: Please, spare me!

He feels the thrust of Spontini's blade, and collapses

bleeding as his attacker flees. The Count is in a daze; thoughts and impressions swim before his vision. He is filled with a strange lightness. Pfitz returns.

PFITZ: Master! Look, he's cut you.

COUNT: It's alright, Pfitz. It isn't deep. Help me to the bed.

PFITZ: My God look at her. I think she's had it. There you are sir, lie down. I'll go and get help.

COUNT: For God's sake, no. Think of the scandal! How would we explain a dead woman on the floor? Get rid of her somehow.

PFITZ: Are you serious?

COUNT: Take her body and dispose of it. Then come back and help me bind up this wound.

Pfitz wraps the wife's body in a blanket and begins to drag her out of the room.

PFITZ: If I'm seen then we'll both be hanged for this, sir!

COUNT: Then don't let yourself be seen.

Those who have wakened by now are still too afraid to leave their rooms, and Pfitz is able to go out without being discovered. He takes the corpse to the river, sometimes carrying it on his shoulder, at other times pulling it behind him, stopping every few minutes to get his breath back and muttering all the while 'Whatever would my father have said about this?' At last he reaches his destination. From the parapet of a bridge, he watches the corpse of the unfortunate woman go falling into the icy water.

Back in the tavern, the guests have dared now to come out from their rooms. Some appear at the Count's door, and cry out with horror.

GUESTS: Murder! An outrage! Look at the great puddle of the poor man's blood, in the middle of the floor.

COUNT: It was Spontini. He killed his wife.

GUESTS: What wife? Who is Spontini? Rest now. We've sent for help.

COUNT: Where's Pfitz? Where's my servant?

160

GUESTS: Now what's he saying? He must be delirious. Who's Pfitz? The Count arrived here alone, he has no servant.

COUNT: Pfitz, don't leave me now.

PFITZ: I'm here again master, it's alright.

GUESTS: Who is he talking to? We see no Pfitz. The poor Count is hallucinating. Is the priest here yet?

PFITZ: Follow me now master. We are going on another journey.

COUNT: I'm coming, Pfitz.

GUESTS: See how he talks to the air! He's fading fast.

CHORUS OF WRITERS:
All that was written
Here is negated.
All that had meaning
Now is undone.
Wrapped in cross-plotting,
The World lies beneath us,
Stories and authors
Merge into one.

COUNT: I hear voices singing, Pfitz. And a fantastic landscape is appearing around us; chasms and mountain gorges are opening up. Are we in Heaven?

PFITZ: Not yet.

A CARTOGRAPHER: Now our final course is charted. Carry us upwards, endless motion of the stars!

COUNT: Can I be dead, Pfitz? It feels no different from being alive.

PFITZ: Are you sure that you still remember what it really felt like to be alive?

Our ascent begins. The air becomes thinner, the sky darker. Cool vapours caress our skin.

COUNT: The world is far below us now. I see the sphere of the earth, so small and blue, like a moist jewel vanishing quickly from sight. Already the orbits of the planets are shrinking beneath us. Stars, and clusters of stars reduced to the faintest dot. How vast! I see a great empty chasm, a bottomless abyss, as if I were held by a thread above the Void with nothing around me but meaningless silence. I feel cold, Pfitz, and frightened.

PFITZ: But master, why should you be afraid of Nothing?

Still we go further.

COUNT: At last! I see shapes appearing out of the darkness.

PFITZ: We have reached the edge of the Universe!

A great mechanism is revealed, consisting of gears, cogs and levers too vast to contemplate, too intricate to comprehend. Everything moves very slowly, and creaks a great deal. It is as if we are inside the workings of a fantastic clock. As we emerge from its furthest side, a new wonder is made visible.

COUNT: What circles are these which now surround us?

PFITZ: The shelves of a great Library. I think we're reaching our own kind of Paradise.

COUNT: I see the stories of my ancestors, made legible to my senses. Volumes are being carried from one place to another; thoughts are being transferred and corrected. This great Library is our final destination. Let us stay here forever, copying out the biographies of my noble family, rewriting and editing the account of our own magnificent journey.

We walk amongst vast shelves, upon which every conceivable thought, impulse or emotion is given expression. To think in this place, or to feel, is simply a matter of selection.

The Library is conical; its galleries focus far above us in a brilliant point of light. We ascend, circle upon circle. And then from behind a row of shelves, a figure appears.

CARTOGRAPHER: Weissblatt?

COUNT: My God, Spontini! Surely he isn't going to kill me again?

Pfitz places himself before the Count as Spontini approaches.

162

PFITZ: Even though neither of us exists, I'm damned if I'll let you kill me!

Spontini easily pushes Pfitz against the railing of the gallery, then picks him up, ready to hurl him over.

COUNT: Spare him!

A shot is heard, and Spontini falls wounded, dropping Pfitz to the floor.

PFITZ: My own father never had such a lucky escape.

Another figure has appeared, holding a pistol.

LEOPOLD: I was one of those who made you, Spontini, and now I bring your story to its conclusion.
SPONTINI: You shall not have the pleasure of rewriting me!

Spontini gets up, clutching his wound, and then launches himself from the gallery. His descent is infinite in magnitude, and though he falls through empty space he does so with a great crashing of thunder.

Now from above, the brilliant light becomes still more intense. A radiant figure is seen hovering, who is named Estrella.

CHORUS OF READERS:
　　　　　Immortal creation of
　　　　　Syllables combining, words redividing
　　　　　In spirals of thought. We read you,
　　　　　We think you, we give you appearance.
　　　　　Yet you will continue
　　　　　Once we are no more.

AN ANGEL (who was Spontini's Wife): Oh joyful peace!
A SECOND ANGEL (who was Frau Luppen): Help me up here, will you? I'm trying to find my husband. Come along now Flussi.

– And what of our Author?
I see now that there is no Author – or else, there are

many Authors, an infinite multitude, so that our story was not one but many, and we ourselves are fictions whose apparent complexity and subtlety of meaning is something which has emerged from simple matter, from the humblest origins. We are a thought which passed through a mind in an instant; a gesture hardly worthy of elucidation.

CARTOGRAPHER: Must I abandon this vision?

LEOPOLD: Only if you wish to go back and live amongst men.

CARTOGRAPHER: It is a difficult choice.

CHORUS LOGICO-PHILOSOPHICUS:
>Whereof we were silent
>Now becomes spoken
>No longer must words
>Stand in place of pure thought.
>Language and meaning
>Are hollow inventions;
>Emergent complexity
>Bear us aloft!

Andrew Crumey was born in Glasgow in 1961. He read theoretical physics and mathematics at St Andrews University and Imperial College, before doing post-doctoral research at Leeds University on nonlinear dynamics. He now lives in Newcastle upon Tyne.

Dedalus published his first novel *Music, in a Foreign Language* to great acclaim in March 1994. It was awarded The Saltire Best First Book Prize.

Andrew Crumey is currently working on his third novel and a collection of short stories.